KILLER TAKE ALL

Also by Philip Race

Self-Made Widow
Johnny Come Deadly

As E.M. Parsons

Dark of Summer
The Easy Gun
Fargo
Texas Heller

KILLER TAKE ALL

PHILIP RACE

CUTTING EDGE

ISBN-13: 978-1-952138-18-8

Published by
Cutting Edge Publishing
PO Box 8212
Calabasas, CA 91372
www.cuttingedgebooks.com

to JERRY PARIS for a variety of things

CHAPTER ONE

The fog lay heavy on the highway. For miles now I'd been creeping along, aiming at the white line in the center of the narrow asphalt road. I had no idea where I was. None at all. And that was a damned uncomfortable feeling for Johnny Berlin, who always liked to know how the game was rigged and where the gimmick lay.

The Ford and I puttered along the winding road, making just enough headway to call it driving. I couldn't see a thing, but the ribbon of white paint led me on.

The fog was a recent development. I'd left the funny little northern California town where I'd spent the night determined to get to Portland, or at least to Salem, before digging in again. Not that I was in any particular hurry.

This road was evidently traveled only by Chinese Seventh Day Adventist Missionaries. And then only in daylight. I hadn't seen a car in hours. Then I saw two.

Both big machines, parked trunk to trunk on the left side of the road. The one pointing toward me had fog lights and I saw them in time to slow. I crept through the swirling fog, blinked my lights to let the guy know I wanted to talk with him. I drifted up beside the two cars, stopped.

A motor roared. I caught a flash of a white face through the window of the first car, then it raced away, motor howling. It disappeared into the fog like a beetle into a hole.

The other car, a green Cadillac, still sat there. I rolled my window down, stuck my head out.

"Hey! How about a little—"

The big car surged forward. I drove my foot down on the accelerator, jumped ahead of the Cadillac. Both of us were just beginning to pick up speed and I stayed in front. It was a very narrow road; he couldn't go around me. I touched my brakes, slewed back and forth, slowing. I couldn't see a thing. Just gray fog. What kept me on the road, I don't know. I stopped slowly, taking the middle of the highway. The guy behind had no choice. He stopped twenty feet back, sat there.

The sound of my shoes scraping on the fog-wet asphalt was loud. As I neared the green car I could see a hand wiping the sweat from the inside of the windshield; he wanted to see me, too.

I peered in the window on the driver's side. There was only one person in the car—a small, dark man with a slash of mustache and a hat shading his upper face. As I looked, he rolled down the window. I found myself looking down the smooth barrel of a very big gun.

"Hey! What's that for?"

"Why did you obstruct me?" The man's voice was treble, had a strange flavor I couldn't identify.

I stiffened, bent over like that, hands held out from my sides. The eyes looking up the barrel of the gun were black as the inside of nothing; they gleamed in the light from the dash.

"Look, mac. All I wanted was some directions. I'm lost. This fog, you know? I'm nobody you need a cannon for, believe me."

"Who are you?"

I straightened. The muzzle followed me.

"Johnny Berlin," I said. "Which I'm sure means nothing to you. I'm just traveling through. I got lost. All I want is someone to show me how to get to Salem. Or Portland. Anywhere they got street lights."

"You are from Portland?"

I figured, what the hell. "Yeah, I'm from Portland."

"You're a liar," the little man said. He waved the gun. "Step back from the door."

I stepped back. He climbed out of the Cad, motioned me ahead of him. We walked to my Ford, still sitting there muttering on the fog-shrouded road. Puffs of exhaust mixed with the gray mist.

"Nevada plates," the little man said.

"Yeah. Look, I lied. I'm sorry. I thought you wanted me to be from Portland. I'm from Vegas, most recently. And Reno. I'm a dealer, a crap dealer. Going to Portland because I've never been there."

"That's the only reason?"

"So help me."

He grunted. "Why were you on this particular road? At this particular time?"

"I told you, mac. I got lost. Believe me, all I want to do is get the hell out of this fog."

"Don't call me mac."

"Yes, sir."

I said "yes sir" because he had a gun. You know a better reason?

"Now step back," he said. "There, on the side of the road, where I can see you. Please do not do anything foolish. I am a nervous man and a coward. I will shoot you."

I believed him. He was a shrimp, about five-six, maybe seven. A good suit draped him and he had manicured nails. He seemed to be about forty or thereabouts. I watched as he carefully shook down the front of the Ford. He found my papers in the glove compartment.

"This is a little-used road, Mr. Berlin." The dark man climbed from the Ford, after riffling through the suits and other stuff in the rear seat. "Not much traffic."

"I'm hip to that," I said.

"Perhaps you are what you claim to be. And then again, perhaps you are something very different."

"Lock. Let me climb in that Ford and I'll shove out of here so fast you'll know I don't care about you. All I need is a direction to go in."

"You know where you are?"

I shook my head, got a cigarette lit now that he had relaxed that gun. "I've been driving in fog since I turned off on this stinking road forty or fifty miles ago."

The little man pushed the gun into a coat pocket. He stood for a moment, head lowered, thinking it over. Then he nodded.

"You are on the Edson Road—the beach road. It is rarely used in this season. You missed the McKaneville cutoff several miles back. Now, where would you like to go?"

"What's this McKaneville? A big town?"

"Fairly large. A lumber port, lumber mills. I'm going in that direction. To Edson. That's about three miles past McKaneville."

I moved closer. His face gleamed wetly in the fog streamers wisping between us. It was a thin face with a sharp chin. The eyes, as I'd suspected, were so dark as to be almost black.

"Let's think about it, huh? I don't want to spend my young life running around in this stuff. And not right next door to the Pacific Ocean for sure. Why don't you let me follow you to this Edson? They got a hotel there?"

"No. Not in Edson. But you could swing around and back a little to McKaneville. From Edson it's quite simple." He studied me for a moment, dipped his sharp chin in a nod. "Righto. I know the road. I'll go ahead. You follow. But not too closely."

"You got a deal."

I shook his hand, stepped on my cigarette. He trotted off to the Cadillac, built-up heels clicking loudly in the cotton-wrapped silence.

And that's how I met Marino Donetti.

Edson was two SLOW signs separated by fifty people. A wide spot. The kind I hate. Every carny has an abnormal fear of very small towns. They're nothing but trouble. You can work your game all over the bigger towns. But hit a village where the whole population turns out for the first grind of the midway, and five gets you fifteen there's a beef before all the tops are pegged down.

Edson was small. Edson had nothing for me. Except the Club Cherbourg which stuck a pink neon twenty feet up into the fog. The Cadillac wheeled off the highway into a graveled parking area immediately in front of a white-and-red Colonial-style building.

Civilization. Any place they got sense enough to charge for liquor I figure is a community.

I got out, locked the Ford. This place looked like liquor and I needed that. The little man stayed in his car. I walked to it, wiggled my fingers at him.

"Thanks."

He rolled the window down. "Not at all. Sorry about the gun. I run a place out the road a piece. The Devil's Play Spot. Carry a bit of money, most times."

"It's all right. Buy you a drink?"

"I think not." His hand strayed beside him to a small tan-leather attaché case on the seat. "I go on here, out the Portland road a few miles. You go this way—" he gestured "—to the next fork. Turn right. Three miles to McKaneville and no way to get off the road."

I started to ask him what had been going on in the middle of the night on a foggy road; two cars and guns and all that jazz. Then I thought about the gun again and decided to mind my own business—which was getting as far away from Las Vegas and a tall leggy redhead named Charlene as possible. I just smiled, started toward the lighted doorway of the nightclub or roadhouse, or whatever it was.

"Oh, Berlin," the little man said. I turned back to the Cad. "Are you looking for work?"

"Work? Well, not particularly, Why?"

"You are a dealer? A gambler?"

"Dealer. Never gambled in my life."

"Yes, of course. This county is quite liberal. You might find employment in this area." He fished for a card, handed it to me through the window. "If you are interested see me at the Devil's Play Spot. Anyone can tell you."

The Club Cherbourg was quite a joint for a whistle-stop town. Four very obviously home-grown musicians made noises on a bandstand set flush against the front of the place, on the right as you entered. A dance floor spread out from the tiny stand; tables surrounded it and blended into the darkness beyond. A bar, canopied in maroon and silver—with spears holding it up— stretched along the left side just past a tiny checkroom. The room was large and softly lit. It might have been San Francisco.

I found a seat at the bar. It wasn't hard. There was only one other person at the bar. And only three or four couples at the tables. I wondered about that because I remembered the service station across the street being loaded with cars. Plus those in the lot. The bartender appeared in front of me. He was a medium specimen with a very black, very straight mustache and watery eyes.

"Yes, sir?"

"This Saturday, mac?"

His eyebrows climbed. "Saturday? Yes, sir, this is Saturday."

"Where is everybody?"

He grinned. "I heard a joke like that once. It had to do with a cockatoo—"

"Yeah, sure." I lit a Camel. "I heard it. Bring me a double, Johnny Walker Red, with water."

He zipped away, came back with the drink. Just then the music stopped and I knew where everyone was. In the comparative silence, I heard the well-remembered chuckle of rolling dice, the low-voiced murmur of a crap game in progress. I paid the mustache. He thanked me, made change. He dropped bills and silver on the bar, leaned forward over the plank.

"Everybody's in the game room." He jerked a thumb toward the far end of the bar.

All I could see were backs. But there was a familiar feel; the gambling aura. Feverish and ripe. Almost a force. Hot game. The room itself was small, holding only the crap table, a twenty-one snap getting absolutely no play, and a green-topped poker table, round and empty in the deeper reaches of the room's rear. The crowd was around the dice table, quiet and interested.

I touched the shoulder of a guy in front of me.

"What's going on?"

The man turned and I caught a flash of irritation and then a big splash of white teeth in a square tanned face.

"I don't know for sure." He increased the grin. "Wish I did. My name's Gurion. I own the place. You care to try?"

He spread his hand toward the crowd.

"Why the mob?" I asked.

He ran a square hand through black hair touched here and there with gray. He shrugged. "Some woman. Having a run of luck. Good advertisement."

But he didn't mean it. His eyes were worried. He caught a murmur from the crowd, a woman's delighted squeal, and forgot about me. I followed him into the crush of onlookers. Being tall has some compensations. I shouldered through a couple layers of people and looked over the heads of the rest.

A nervous brunette, very well dressed, was shooting. The table was what is known in the trade as a California double-dealer. That means that two people work identical layouts on either side of the stickman. This one was a little different, however. The backline barred ace-deuce instead of double-ace or double-six; the propositions all read "for one" instead of "to one." As percentages go, this layout was lethal. If anyone was managing to beat this game, I wanted to see it.

The brunette swept the dice down the table and a subdued murmur arose.

"Sixes, two—crap twelve, she threw," the stickman said. He was a young Indian-looking joker in shirt sleeves, wearing a worried expression.

A girl worked the box. Calling her just girl was a little like calling Whirlaway just horse. She was blonde, with a face like they launched all those ships for back in Troy. She had hair so blonde it was almost white and it capped her head like lemon froth. Her skin was deeply tanned and her body, what I could see of it over the table, was trim and complete. As I inventoried her, she reached over the layout, stacked twenty-nine chips on the one the nervous brunette had on the thirty-for-one crap twelve. Her hand trembled slightly. She frowned, looking out over the crowd. Our eyes met for an instant and held. She looked perplexed and very lovely. I smiled and she turned back to the game.

She was a real doll. But cold. She was classic beauty fastened together with loving care, each piece being more perfect than the last; built to excite and delight and maybe enslave. And then frozen, the whole thing. There was a coldness about her you could feel.

The brunette shot again, won with a natural. I'd seen enough. The stickman couldn't handle it.

A hand on my bicep spun me. The woman facing me filled slacks and blouse like they should be filled. She wore a dealer's apron of pool-table green. Her lips were smiling and she seemed glad to see me. It took a moment, then I remembered.

"Bev," I said. "Bev King. Haven't seen you since Tahoe. How are things?"

"Big Johnny Berlin," the girl said. "Still pretty and still stuck-up. What are you doing around here?"

I pulled her out of the crowd. She gripped my arm against one swelling breast and walked, smiling up at me.

"For one thing," I said, "I'm watching this joint go broke."

She stopped. "What did you say, Johnny?"

"The scuffler." I nodded at the table. "She'll milk your rack dry. The way that dealer goofs, tomorrow this place'll be under new management."

She almost fainted.

CHAPTER TWO

BEV KING was nice people. A carnival brat, she'd graduated naturally to dealing and had worked some of the real good spots around the country. I couldn't see her in a joint like the Club Cherbourg. I'd known Bev on and off for some time. At one time we'd had a short but torrid romance. She was my kind of girl; full-bodied and generous, not demanding and very wise. Hip, you might say. The thing hadn't lasted long.

Right now she would be about thirty-five. She'd got married, had a couple of kids before the war made her a widow.

Anyway, she worked hard, and wore no man's collar. Quite a girl. We found a table, got drinks. She really needed one.

"This's real cozy, honey," I said when we were settled. "But I have to make it to McKaneville, or some such."

"Johnny, listen." She took a gulp of her drink. "You got to help me."

I grinned, took her hand. Her hair, so dark it was blue in the low light, framed her face and made the milky pallor more pale by contrast. She shook her hand loose.

"No, Johnny. Be serious."

I sat back. She was hacked about something, all right. She fidgeted with the front of her blouse, pulling the silk tight over her fine breasts.

"Can you do something about that woman? Can you, Johnny? Can you stop her?"

"Can I what?" That shocked me. I got a cigarette going while I got behind that one. "Can I stop her? Why the hell should I want to?"

"For me, Johnny. You've got to." She leaned forward. "Is there anything you could do if you wanted to?"

"Well, sure." I stared at my cigarette. "But why? I'm a hustler myself."

"Johnny, listen." She gripped my arm. "You got to take the stick and stop that woman. It'll break Dan. He can't—"

"Wait a minute," I said. "Now I get it, maybe. The wide guy? With all the teeth?"

She nodded, miserable. Her eyes dropped and her hands tore a cigarette to pieces, scattered the crumbs on the white cloth.

"Yes," she said, real low. "But don't say anything, Johnny. He's married. And—well, it's all a mess."

"What do you know."

"Please, Johnny—"

"Why doesn't Gurion do something? It's none of my look in, kid. You know that."

"I know, I know. But, look—Dan had a dealer. A good one. Ford Messner. They had an argument about some organization or other and Ford quit. The only dealer around was Jack Kilgallen. The kid in there. And he knows from nothing."

Her fine dark eyes were wet at the corners. I could never remember seeing her like that before. This jerk Gurion really had her on the hook.

"Let me tell you how it is," she said. "Will you?"

"Tell," I said. "Stories I always like."

She wet her lips, said, "Dan hasn't got a dime. Not really. He and Lucy have been married for about ten years. The club's hers. In her name. Dan was a sawyer in a mill downtown when he met her. She had a tavern. You know, beer, poker—that bit? Anyway, they hooked up, worked hard together and finally wound up with the Cherbourg. But they don't ring up enough to make a living for themselves and the three kids."

"What's that got to do with losing a couple bucks in a crap game? Jesus, they can't be playing it that close."

"Listen. Dan is trying to pay off the note, get the business straightened around so that he and Lucy can get a divorce. She feels the same way, been playing around for years. But right now a split leaves Dan with beans. And he's not a beans guy. He wants to take care of Lucy and the kids and still have enough left so he and I can have a couple good years."

She looked at her drink, pushed it away. Her eyes were blank and shadowed. I didn't say anything.

"Haven't I got 'em coming, Johnny? A couple good ones?" She shook her head, attacked another cigarette with nervous fingers. "Then that damned Donetti comes around with his association action and Messner quits. He used to draw trade. Now this."

"You said Donetti. How does he figure?"

"Johnny, about the game. Will you—"

"Tell me about Donetti."

She took a breath. "All right. Marino Donetti owns the big place out at Devil's Lake. He wants to get all the owners together in a sort of protective association to resist outside pressure from other interests to syndicate the area. Or something like that. Messner was for it. Dan isn't. Neither are Paul Carter and a couple of the other club owners. That's it. They've been growling and muttering at each other for months. Dan says we can outsit them. But he's running short on dough."

"He could close down the table."

She looked at me scornfully. "You know better than that. This is a walk-in trap. We get the same people all the time. Close it once 'cause somebody's winning and there goes your action from now on. You could stop it, Johnny. If you wanted to."

"Bev, go get this Dan of yours. I'll give him a hand—if he wants it."

"Oh, Johnny." She got up and ran around to me. "I knew you would," she said happily and kissed me. "You won't be sorry."

I pushed her toward the curtained doorway. "I'm sorry already."

She walked away. I lit another Camel and mentally booted myself for getting in the middle of what had all the appearances of a sticky situation. Then I watched Bev make her way across the floor and decided it might be worth it. She sure looked good walking away.

Dan Gurion wasn't pleased with me. He was the guy I'd talked to in the game room; still wide and toothy. He wore a light, some-kind-of-tweed sport coat. I put him about forty-five, forty-eight—older than he liked to think he looked. He had on thick-framed horn-rimmed glasses. Bev hovered in attendance.

"Mr. Berlin," the man said, extending his hand.

I shook it. He sat and we looked at each other for a moment. Then he said, "Well..."

I said, "Well..."

Bev grabbed glasses, left hastily with, "I'll get some drinks."

Dan Gurion's eyes were wary and a trifle hard and the politician's smile was gone. He looked me over good. I did him the same favor over the rim of my glass.

He said, "There's not much use in talking around it, Mr. Berlin. Bev tells me I'd better do something about the situation in the game room. She also tells me that you are the man who can do it."

"I am," I agreed. "If I want to. Right now I'm wondering what the guy you got dealing is going to say. I'll have to take over the game to do you any good."

He brushed it aside. "Kilgallen's not important. What is important is stopping these people from walking off with my club. Can you do that?"

Bev came with the drinks. I grinned at her, took the glass of whisky.

"I can do it."

Then Gurion walked back into the game room.

Soon after Jack Kilgallen, the deposed dealer, stormed out of the doorway and up to the bar. His face was dark and he looked like someone had told him Custer had really defeated Sitting Bull.

I slid into the pit, tapped Dan Gurion on the shoulder. He turned. "Oh, there you are, Johnny." He said to the girl, "Fran, this is Johnny. He'll deal."

"Fran," I said, and smiled around the table. "People. Shall we go on?"

The game went on.

I took the stick and dealt it automatically. It felt good to be directing a game again. I was very much aware of the blonde girl beside me. A subtle perfume, like sunny grass, drifted to me. I smiled at her, nodded. She pulled my head down, whispered in my ear.

"These people. Are you going to stop them?"

She smelled good and her hand was soft. There was a tiny line between her brows. "I am, indeed," I said, and waited for the chance.

The layout captured my full attention. I let the sweep and power of the eternal lust to gamble pull me into the contest and I handled the table with a sure, deft touch developed over too many tables and too many years. Before the dice got around to the dark sharpie, I glimpsed admiration in Fran's eyes.

The nervous doll with the educated fingers grabbed the dice in her turn and rubbed them between her palms. The script had changed. Now she bet a stack of blues on the front line. She shot, caught ten for a point. She shouldn't have done that. She took the odds for the same amount they had on the line. It was the biggest single bet of the evening. My blonde assistant leaned toward me.

"She's playing the limit, you know," she whispered.

I winked, chattered up the action. The dark girl rubbed the dice, got them fixed in her fancy fingers for the throw.

I said, "Just a minute, lady." I raised the stick, stopped the game. "See that the dice jump over the stick, please?" I reached out, laid the wicker hook on the layout three-quarters of the way downtable. "Both dice to the wall."

She looked at me incredulously, started to protest. I just shook my head, told her to shoot. She rubbed the dice and looked at me again, a sharp glance full of frustration. She had quite a bundle down. But even at that she would walk out with a hundred bucks of Cherbourg money if she quit after this roll. Which I was sure she would do.

"Over the stick and home, lady. Make ten for the people."

She shot. She couldn't slide, of course. Not with the stick laying there. The dice hully-gullied down the table, bounded off the rubber. Ace and a trey, four easy.

I said, "Four, easy—hunting ten. After four, come some more. Field roll, the comes go."

I fished some busters out of my coat pocket, gripped them flat-handed, wedged between the thumb fat and the outside edge of my palm. I picked up the fronts with the same hand when the stick dragged them up, made the easy drop-switch. Then I gave the svelte shotmaker the busters and she knew I'd fed her. She knew, all right. The switch is impossible to detect, but the move is easy enough to see. If you knew what to look for. I dropped the fronts, the square dice, in my side pocket, showed the girl some teeth.

She'd play hell making ten. One cube had aces, treys and fives; the other deuces, fours and sixes.

She threw the dice spitefully and the red cubes came up seven. An excited murmuring arose from the players, most of whom had been riding the girl's hot hand.

I sang, "Four—trey, she went away. The last good comes and the don'ts to pay. A new shooter."

The feeling of the game lightened. And gradually it became just another crap game, not life and death on every roll. I leaned toward the blonde.

"I'm Johnny Berlin," I said. "Who're you?"

She looked up; our eyes were only inches apart. Her face flushed under my frank gaze, turned away.

She said, "Fran. Fran Cole."

A real doll. I began to wonder if I might possibly break my lifetime rule about small towns. After all, Portland had nothing for me. Another table, another game.

The dice tumbled.

About two-thirty the action tailed off and we closed the game. I stood still for congratulations from Bev and Dan. Fran Cole took off as soon as the action died. I got away from the mob, ducked through the curtains after her.

I ran into Jack Kilgallen.

CHAPTER THREE

The cool bar towel eased the ache in my temple. There was a dull, thick feeling under my right eye. I'd have a mouse in the morning to keep my broken knuckle company.

"Hold still," Bev demanded. Her lush body pinned me to the bar as she held the towel to my head.

I winced and leaned back. On the floor, Jack Kilgallen lay where my desperation punch had put him moments before. Condi Capucho, the bartender, held a towel full of ice on the kid's eye. Dripping bar towels all over the joint.

Dan Gurion came from the stairway door. He took in the tableau, walked to the bar.

"What happened?" he asked.

"Little Beaver," I said. "He took exception to me moving him out. I tried to tell him it was just for the evening. But he wouldn't have any."

Bev pushed on the towel and I jerked my head away.

"Hey. You trying to stick that thing in my ear?"

"I'll stick it in your big fat mouth if you don't hold still."

Fran Cole slid onto the stool next to me at the bar. Bev smiled at her, went back to torturing me with the wet towel.

"You seem to be a man of many talents, Mr. Berlin," the blonde girl said.

She had changed her costume. Now she wore a light dress of pale blue that accentuated the deep tan of her neck and shoulders, pointed up the whiteness of her hair. Her eyes were startling; deep, deep violet in the light.

"I am indeed," I said. I pushed Bev away. "Give me a break, Bev."

"Berlin, I'd like to talk to you about working for me," said Gurion.

"No, thanks," I replied. "Too small a town for me."

Fran Cole said, "You haven't seen McKaneville, Mr. Berlin. It's loads bigger than Edson. Lots going on. You might think about it. There may be more to see than you know."

She turned on the stool and I got a good look at her trim body, slimming to flaring hips, neat thighs. I looked her over deliberately. She flushed under my examination, a line appearing between her eyes.

"You could be right," I told her.

Her lips thinned and she turned away. I turned back to Gurion.

"Look, Gurion. I appreciate the offer. But Laughing Boy there'll make you a good dealer. If he wises up a little. Me, I'm gone for Portland."

"I could make you a percentage deal. How's that? Say thirty per cent." His eyes slid away. "Of the net, of course."

Nothing wrong with this guy's arithmetic. I laughed, fished for a cigarette.

"No, thanks. I'll make it to McKaneville tonight, get a start for Portland tomorrow. I can't stand small towns."

Condi Capucho, the bartender, spoke from the floor. "He's coming around, Dan. His eyes just came open."

Kilgallen came awake, groaning. He sat up with the bartender's help. I turned back to the bar, watched Fran mix drinks. I heard Dan and Condi get the kid out of the joint. Dave paid him off, fired him. I felt bad about that.

Fran leaned on the bar gloomily.

"Oh, come on. What is this? A funeral? Life goes on. Have a drink and then I'll drive you home, huh? Sound all right? Maybe we can stop somewhere for coffee."

"I have a car, thank you." She pressed fingertips to her temples, shook her head once. "I'm really very tired."

Gurion came back and I swung around to him. "Dan, you shouldn't have fired that kid. I told you I didn't want the job. I wasn't kidding."

"All right, Berlin." He got on a stool, gripped his drink. His eyes looked tired and the lines around the wide mouth were deep and shadowed. He nodded. "I'll find somebody. But not him. These games are too important. Without the revenue from the game room, I can't make it. It's touch and go as it is."

"Yeah, well, I'm sorry." I turned to the bar. "Look, it's none of my business and I'm butting out. But strictly. The joke is over. Now, how do I get to McKaneville?"

Dan said, "Just follow the road, bear right. Try the Hotel Kenyon. It's reasonable and clean."

I walked to the door with Fran, still not convinced I couldn't talk her into something. We jammed up there, saying good-nights. Someone mentioned that I should turn right at the Club Carroll onto the Clover Canyon Road for the quickest route to the hotel.

Fran climbed into her heap with a neat display of stocking. Her legs were slim and nicely rounded. She closed the door, rolled down the window.

"Good night," she said.

"You're making a mistake, lady. Such sterling tales of derring-do I could recount." I grinned at her. "Just think, a cup of instant coffee and holding hands over a greasy table. Doesn't that sound exciting?"

"You kill 'em, don't you, Berlin?" The eyes, murky blue-violet in the car's shadow searched my face. She didn't smile.

"Yeah," I said, leaning in. "I do, indeed." I looked at her for a long moment, trying to read the expression I'd seen for a fleeting instant on that smooth face. She looked away. "You're afraid," I said softly. "That's the bit. You're scared to death."

"Get away from the door," she said tightly. Her toe stabbed the accelerator and the coupe tore out of there, rapping my fingers hard against the doorpost. She almost didn't make the corner. Then she got it straightened; the tail lights dissolved into the fog. I stood there for a couple of minutes after the sound of the coupe had died. My fingers stung from the impact of the doorpost. I trudged to my car.

It was an interesting situation I'd fallen into. During the evening Fran had brought me up to date on the local gossip. The gambling was Vegas-style; pay a tax on your table and go. Consequently, with all the logging and lumber mills, the area was a potential gold mine. Just lately a force for the forming of a cartel, a Gambler's Protective Association, had been giving all the owners headaches. It sounded to them like syndication. The prime mover was Marino Donetti. I said nothing about having met the man. His odd behavior on the road took on added significance with the story.

The dealer Dan had lost, Ford Messner, was reputed to be Donetti's right hand. But it was just talk because he had gone to work just down the road a piece from Cherbourg after leaving Gurion—a place called Coley's.

My headlamps picked out a Y sign on the side of the road on the outskirts of McKaneville. The fog had lifted some, now hovering twenty feet or so over the road. Visibility was much better. I saw a glow of diffused light through the murk from the area within the spread of the Y. A small neon sign said Club Carroll in red tubing. This was Carter's after-hours joint that Condi had mentioned. The rendezvous where the hustlers and dealers, bartenders and late crawlers gathered to cut up touches. Paul Carter was supposed to be an ex-gambler.

The fog hugged the road only here and there and I made pretty good time for a mile or so. Then I picked up a tail. The suits and stuff hanging behind me on the car rack made it hard to tell. But a pair of headlamps had been gaining on me steadily. I pushed the Ford a little and the lights kept pace. Then I slowed down, decided to let the joker go around me.

Before I could spit a hurtling black mass nudged my inside rear fender. I wrenched the wheel, got a rubber squeal from the tires and shot way out on the wrong side of the road. I rammed my foot down on the gas, fought the wheel. The dark car, its lights blinding me as I turned my head, slid inside between my Ford and the canyon wall. Our fenders touched with a grinding tear. I fought the wheel desperately and slammed in front of the other car, shot up the side of the canyon wall. Metal screeched as the Ford rode the wet dirt. My speed kept me rolling. I bounced down to the asphalt, tore into the next curve like a racer.

It was a hairpin, turning in, the outer lip dropping away to black and menacing emptiness. My tires scrambled for traction and I almost made it. Way out on the rim of the gully the fierce momentum took the little Ford. While I hung there fighting for control, the black car rammed through on the inside and crunched against my right front fender.

For a split second everything in the world was suspended in time, even the yell of protest in my throat. I heard the guard rail pop very distinctly. And then I knew I was going over; there was nothing under the Ford and I tensed with the half-helpless feeling you get when you begin a half-gainer off a high board.

Some forgotten instinct shoved my foot under the brake pedal; my hands gripped the wheel, stiff-armed my body back against the seat. The car rolled and rolled in the air. I felt the first bounce. And the second. Then something slapped the side of my head and I went out.

✤   ✤   ✤

I opened my eyes. I was twisted in the front part of my Ford. It was upside down. The roof met the tops of the doors; there was no window space left. The mass of metal was still settling. I hadn't been out long. I kicked a hole through the floorboards, climbed out and dropped to the rocky floor of the canyon. The gully was shallow at this point. My roll had ended thirty or forty feet from the road. The Ford smoked; one headlight still burned. Wisps of fog reached downward from the roadside and the light brushed them aside. I felt myself for broken bones, could find none. Just my nose. It was a mess. There was blood all over my suit.

Twin streaks of light shot out over the gully from the lip of the canyon above. I moved around the wreck, got out of the light. I didn't know who that was up there.

"Anybody hurt down there?" It was a woman's voice.

"No," I said. It was pretty squeaky, but the woman heard me.

"Shall I call an ambulance?" the voice inquired.

"Don't call anybody," I said. "I'll be right up. You can take me to town."

I walked to the front of the Ford, put the headlight out with a rock. Then I started up the steep side of the gully. It took everything I had to. make it. I hauled myself the last few feet, crawled through the broken opening in the guard rail, and fell forward on the wet asphalt.

Someone was talking. I opened my eyes and there in front of me appeared the most wonderful pair of female legs I have ever seen. Or ever hope to see, for that matter. A very beautiful, dark woman with a belted trench coat and no hat stood above me. Her mouth was full and a little petulant. Her hair, whipped by the rising wind, was darker than shoe polish.

"Are you hurt? Do you feel any pain?"

I grunted, sat up. "I heard a joke like that once. It went—"

"Please," the woman said. "Get up and I'll take you to the hospital."

Her hands wormed under my arms, lifted. I stood, looked down at her. She had a rounded face, pale and evenly featured. Her eyes were light-colored.

"No hospital," I said. "But I'll take the ride."

"What happened?"

We started for the car, her arm around me. Her body was soft where it touched me. She reminded me of Bev, firm yet yielding, curved where it counted.

I said, "I don't know. Lost control, I guess."

I saw that she was headed in the same direction I'd been going; she wouldn't have seen the dark car. We climbed into her car, a green Cadillac, and started for town.

Neither of us said anything. She drove and I rested. I told her the Kenyon Hotel and she took me there. The last couple of blocks I rolled my head on the seat back, watched the play of light on the woman's firmly molded breasts pushing aside the opened trench coat as she spun the wheel. The dark dress strained upward with each breath and her rounded arms flashed olive-dark in the light from the car's dash. An unreasoning thickness grabbed my throat.

That's me. Aching from a car wreck, mind whirling with speculation, in a car with a complete stranger. And still I couldn't keep my eyes off her after the first look. I didn't know then that a gift to incite an unexplainable physical excitement in every man was this woman's peculiar possession. One look and you thought of going to bed with her. Just like that.

We stopped in front of the Kenyon Hotel. The woman twisted around in the seat to face me and the weak light from the lobby streamed through her hair.

"You sure you're all right?" she asked. "Mister ..."

"Berlin," I said quickly. "Johnny Berlin."

"Johnny Berlin." Her voice was perfectly controlled, a light contralto. "Are you going to be around, Johnny? I'd like to see you without lumps."

"I'll be around," I said. It sounded grim. "What's your name? I'd like to know who to thank."

"Gina," she said. "Gina Donetti. Good night, Mr. Berlin."

It was ten minutes after four. I got a room, told the clerk to call a garage about my car and went to the phone booth. The operator got Dan Gurion's home for me. The phone rang for a while, then Dan's deep voice came over the wire.

"Gurion..."

"Dan? Johnny Berlin. Listen—that deal you mentioned. Is it still open?"

"Open? Why sure, Johnny," the nightclub owner said. "I'll be very happy to make a deal with you. What changed your mind?"

"You don't know, huh?"

"I haven't any idea. But I'm glad." He chuckled. "Probably Fran Cole. She is a doll."

"Yeah. Well, that isn't it. Someone tried to kill me after I left your place. I figure I'll stay around in case he wants to try again."

I hung up on his shocked silence.

CHAPTER FOUR

The next day, I went to Portland. But it was just a quick trip and Dan Gurion came along. I'd given him one reason for going; we needed dice and cards and some decent entertainment to build up the club. We'd had a big hassle over that. What I really went for was a gun. I bought one first thing.

Portland was wet and seemed very dull to me. They had just had a clean-up, one of the periodic drives at the gambling and vice. Made me glad I'd stayed in McKaneville. Or at least dulled my frustration. We stayed overnight, did business by phone and by noon Monday we were burrowing through the moisture-laden air on our way back toward McKaneville.

We had hired an instrumental trio fresh from an engagement at a top San Francisco supper club. For a feature we had really gone overboard. Laddy Layton, latest of the scintillating emotion purveyors, had played his latest date at a local theater and was free for three weeks. Actually it was a terrific break getting him. A freak in his schedule. The price was too much for a place like the Cherbourg but I twisted Dan's arm and we signed him. I knew damned well he'd pack the club. I didn't like him myself. But he killed the people.

When we got back to my hotel, Dan suggested slyly that I have a look around at some of the other clubs in the neighborhood.

I got the point immediately.

"Dan, I told you. I'm not messing in your hassle with Donetti and the Gambler's Protective Association. That's your worry. I'll run your game and make you money. That's it. I'm not a cop and I'm no Sir Galahad. I'll say this, though. If this thing touches the reason someone wrecked my car, tried to kill me, then maybe you'll find out something. But I'm not snooping on purpose. I'm looking for no holes in my pretty head."

"You see my point," he said. "I can't stand for being victimized into joining something that will dictate my future business policy. And that's what Donetti wants. What he's wanted from the first. We've never needed to organize before. Then he moves in with that big operation at the lake and suddenly we need to protect ourselves against outside interests. They'll have to fight me."

"What I'd like," I said, "is to find out why in the hell someone wanted to push me. And I will."

Gurion's brow furrowed. His hands tightened on the wheel. "I wish you'd look around, Johnny. I'm over my head and I know it."

I grunted. "If Donetti's syndicate-backed, you are. And so am I. If that's the case, I'll run like a dog. And you'll join whatever they tell you to join."

I pushed the cylinder of the gun I'd bought, spun it on my palm.

"I need this year bad, Johnny. I've worked all my life. Cutting trees, setting chokers. I worked up to sawyer and that's what I'd still be if it hadn't been for Lucy. She had a little money, a little tavern. We got married. I never did love her. Not the way I love Bev. All we've had was the business. And the kids. I can't break away and leave her nothing. I owe her too much. And now there's Bev…"

"She's a good one," I said softly.

He nodded, said nothing.

"Okay, Dan. I'll look around tonight—after I have a talk with young Sitting Bull. You set everything up like we planned. And don't worry. Tomorrow night we hang 'em from the rafters."

He smiled, all the teeth jumping out white and square and strong. The glasses made him look owlish. Then he sobered.

"You figure out a way, Johnny," he said. "I'm with you till my breath runs out."

My room had been tidied somewhat. My bags were unpacked. Suits hung in the closet in orderly ranks and my shoes gleamed at me from the rug. I signed a chit to valet service for ten dollars and fell into a hot tub. And forgot about the whole mess in the fragrant heat and soothing steam.

Except Gina Donetti. I didn't forget about her. Only one thing would fix that.

Out of the tub, I called the desk and left instructions for a car to be hired for me. Then I dressed. Carefully, utilizing the best of my wardrobe. The suit was one I'd had made in Hollywood. A flannel, dark gray. White shirt, narrow tie, black shoes. I thought about the girl in the green Cadillac and marveled at the completely silly flash of jealousy I felt in thinking of her and the little man with the gun.

I picked up my keys, comb and wallet from the bureau. The .38 winked at me from the handkerchief drawer. My hand reached for it. I thought about what a bulge it would make in my manly beauty. Gina wouldn't want a bulgy guy, now would she? A small penknife with a tiny sharp blade that I used to trim my nails lay among the clutter. I slipped it in my pocket.

For protection. Joke. I laughed all the way down in the creaky elevator. Oh, you're a funny fellow, Berlin. You kill me.

Damn near did.

I drove around in the rented heap getting acquainted. A mile or so south of town I found a tiny roadside lunchroom, stopped. A dumpy waitress rustled my order while I got change, dropped a dime in the phone on the wall, dialed Fran's number.

When the connection was made, I said, "Fran? This is Johnny Berlin."

Her voice was just as I'd remembered it, clear and unaffected. And sort of deep for a woman.

She said, "Oh, yes. The funny fellow. You're still around, I see."

"Easy with the sarcasm, honey. I'm your boss as of now."

"Yes, I heard." She stopped, the line carrying only the soft sound of her breathing. Then, "I'm trying to figure if I like that or not."

"Look," I said finally. "What I wanted to tell you was that Dan and I went to Portland."

"I know that too. And that you've made a deal to run his games. And that you had an accident last night. And that you and Bev King used to be an item in what is referred to as the good old days."

I took a breath. Small towns. Everybody knows everything about everyone else.

"If you know so much, maybe you know who tried to kill me? Who ran me off the highway?"

"Tried to—" Her breath whooshed out and suddenly the strain was gone. Her voice became anxious. "Are you joking, Johnny?"

"It was for real, but nobody knows it wasn't just an accident. Except Dan and me. And the guy who drove the car that nudged me."

"But what for, Johnny? Did you know anyone in town? Are you in trouble?"

"Not that I know of. Look, forget it. I'll take care of it. We got some talent in Portland. Tomorrow we open with a bang. The Cherbourg's new policy goes into effect."

"I'm glad," she said. But there was no interest. "Johnny, where are you? What are you doing tonight?"

"Is that a proposition?"

"Johnny, listen. Some very funny things have been happening in this town lately. I've lived here all my life and never have I felt such an undercurrent of violence. Maybe you better not stay around here. Maybe you—"

"Maybe you're grinding someone else's ax, beautiful."

She said nothing. And I had nothing to say. I didn't even have a good reason for calling her in the first place.

"Johnny?"

"Yes?"

"This Association thing. Do you know anything about it? It's all over town," she said. "You and Donetti. The story says you're his strongarm man."

This was a switch. A story like that would make a fine cover for someone who was out to get me. But why me?

Into the phone I said, "Do you believe that?"

"I don't know what to believe." She drew a deep breath, magnified by the phone connection. "I usually just mind my own business. This time..."

"This time?"

"Nothing. I'll see you. Johnny—" I felt the hesitation. "Be careful," she said.

"I'll be careful. And the way I feel right now, somebody better watch me."

I hung up, threw the pudgy waitress a dollar and got out of there. Food no longer appealed to me.

It was just growing dark. A faint haze came over the coast hills from the direction of the ocean. I stood in the cindered parking area and got a cigarette lit. A neon sign popped, buzzed into life over my head. I walked to the car.

It was a plain, black Ford two-door sedan. I had the door open before I noticed anything wrong. And then it was too late.

"Get in. And be careful. This thing's loaded."

He was big, even sitting the way he was, slumped in the back seat. And ugly. His voice was like metal on concrete. A flat, oily shine came from the forty-five in his hand.

"What is this?"

"You don't care what it is. You don't care anything except you don't make me shoot you." He leaned forward into the light and I saw a scarred; lumpy-nosed face and shoulders like a young horse. "Now get in, fella, and drive like I tell you. We're going to see a man."

CHAPTER FIVE

Cooley's Club was on the beach road about a mile beyond the Cherbourg. It sat alone on the gray asphalt, a rustic porch and a dark-blue neon. Beer signs were tacked on the weathered front. Across the road the bay lapped a rocky shore. There were no other buildings close enough to see. It was dark now and the fog had begun to drift. Coley's Club. Not exactly the Stork.

The goon walked me right in the front door. I saw a leather-and chrome-stripped bar, a huge fireplace with a log fire burning in it. Several couples filled the overstuffed pieces strewn round the fire. A barmaid worked the stick for a handful of early customers. My guide pushed me down a hallway to the left of the bar. There was a blue bulb burning over a door. The hallway was dark except for the single light. I slid my hand into my pocket, gripped the little knife. I don't know what I thought I could do with it, but I felt less naked with the two-inch blade opened, the whole thing palmed half up my sleeve.

The room under the blue light was an office. It was furnished with a worn rug and an old-fashioned, leather chaise longue, a beat-up oak desk and a wooden file cabinet. To the right, a door led out to the parking area in the rear. I could see light glinting off the cars through the slits of the blind.

A skinny guy in a black suit that looked like it had been cut for somebody else sat behind the desk. Coley O'Rourke. The goon grabbed my arm, muscled me up to the desk. I wrenched away.

"Keep your hands off or I'll make you use that gun."

I saw the quick shine leap into the ape's dull eyes. I wished I had a gun. A pretty, new one, for instance, like the one keeping my handkerchiefs company in a bureau drawer.

O'Rourke said, "Mops!" and the goon stopped. "Pat him. But do it easy."

He settled back with a frosty smile as the ape ran his big hands over me. He touched everywhere.

"He's clean."

"Fine. Bring me the gun."

Mops moved warily around me, walked to the chair and handed the forty-five to his boss. Maybe it was the only one they had.

"Things are tough all over," I said.

O'Rourke slammed the gun into a drawer, making a show of it.

He said, "Mops, go tell Ford I want to see him."

The ape left. I got a cigarette out and lit up, careful the knife didn't show. I wondered if I should take the guy now or wait and see what developed. I decided to wait.

I said, "You know anything about my long trip down the short gully the other night?"

He smiled. "I heard about it. Made me very happy."

The big man came back then. With a slender man in a neat suit and a maroon shirt and no tie. He had brown hair and pure white eyebrows. The eyes were cold. Ford Messner. No one had to tell me that.

"Come in, Ford. Here's that Berlin."

The crap dealer nodded, leaned against the wall to my left. He flipped three half-dollars over each other in one long-fingered hand. He said nothing. O'Rourke leaned back.

"Okay, sharpie. What's your story? What's your business in McKaneville? Who sent for you?"

"My business is my own, O'Rourke. You want to play gangster, get somebody else for a straight man."

The nightclub owner's sallow skin reddened and his lip lost some of the droop. His sharp chin lifted.

"All right," he said. "We can save some time. We know who you are and what you came for. Mops saw you and Donetti outside the Cherbourg Saturday night. That means he called for help from his big-time friends because we're bucking him on his Protective Association. That smells like syndicate to me. You smell like syndicate to me. You tell us what you're supposed to do—what Donetti has in mind—and you might not get hurt."

I studied my cigarette end. O'Rourke waited. I could hear the ape breathing noisily behind me. Messner didn't change expression. His coins flicked, flicked.

"You got nothing to say, is that it?"

I sighed. "You catch on quick. Answer me a question and I'll tell you all you want to know. Who pushed me over that canyon Saturday night?"

"You're in no position to bargain. Show him, Mops."

It was too sudden. I expected a little talk first. But the big guy's hand exploded behind my ear like a ball bat. I fell, dropping the knife. My head cracked the desk front. Somebody yelled. I pushed against the floor, got to my knees. My hand touched the blade of the knife on the floor and I fumbled it into a tight grip. Mops stood beside me, looking down. I grabbed his belt and heaved myself upright. He cocked a huge fist and I slashed blindly with the knife. The blade caught him high in the shoulder, ripped downward across his arm.

He screamed like a girl and reached with his other hand. Bright red leaped from the gaping cut; threads of blue cloth dangled into the wound. He tried to press the gash closed. I pivoted on my heel and pulled the little knife across his belly, low down. It was a tiny knife. And that saved him. He stumbled backward, an unbelieving expression on his face. The chaise hit at his knee and he fell upon it.

Messner hadn't moved. His coins flipped a little faster, maybe. O'Rourke looked sick. He had the forty-five in his yellow hand, gripped loosely. I shook my head, got my feet under me. Then I stepped around the desk, slapped O'Rourke on the mouth. The gun thudded to the floor.

"You—you cut him," he said.

"You're clever." I turned to watch Messner. He still leaned against the wall. "I'll see you, O'Rourke. And if I find you had anything to do with running me into that ditch I'll put a bullet in you."

I walked by Ford Messner. He still leaned negligently on the wall, flipping coins. I said, "I think you and I should talk."

He nodded slightly. Mops lay on the couch, moaning deep in his throat. Blood was shiny on the brown leather.

I went out through the club; no one even noticed me. I got in the car, started it. A figure stepped from the shadows. Ford Messner. He walked efficiently. The way he did everything. He stopped at the car.

"We called a doctor for Parisi," he said. His voice was flat, neither deep nor high. "I'll see you at the Carroll after two. Know where it is?"

I nodded. He turned away. Then he stopped, a thin smile touching his lips.

"With you around, man, someone's liable to get killed. Try to see it isn't you."

I could see the bit now. The fact that I'd arrived at the Cherbourg with Donetti had started everyone speculating. One of them had decided to do something about it. That eliminated Kilgallen from the list as far as the car business went. Or so I figured it. He'd been dealing when Donetti and I arrived in the fog. I stopped at a drugstore in Edson, called the Devil's Play Spot. A desk clerk got me Gina.

"Mrs. Donetti? This is Johnny Berlin."

"Oh, yes." The voice was soft and full of woman. "Of course. How are you, Mr. Berlin?"

"I'm fine. Look, I want to talk to you. How about the Club Carroll some time in the next couple of hours?"

She hesitated. Then she said, "I can't imagine what you'd have to say to me. But—if you like."

"You know what I have to say," I said, and hung up before she decided to play games.

I found a stool near the door of the Carroll. Easy to see why Carter got all the business. It was a nice place.

"Here you are," the barman said, sliding my drink in front of me. He studied me a moment. Then he said, "Your name Berlin?"

"Yeah. Why?"

"Guy called here a couple of times. Tried to get you. He left a message. Just a minute."

The barman went to the register, came back with a small slip of paper. His eyes touched mine, slid away. He seemed nervous. Like someone had told him I was a salesman for Asiatic Flu.

"Says call Marino Donetti at this number."

A man slid onto the stool next to mine, turned to me with a cheerful grin. He was thirty-some, medium all over. His cheeks were full and seemed polished. He wore a tie that would have been loud on Central Avenue in L.A. Here it was downright boisterous. I grinned back at him. I couldn't help it.

"Hi," he said.

"Hello there. Want a drink?"

He grinned harder. "Yeah. Don't mind. But look here, champ. What would you say to a hundred bucks?"

"Hello."

"Yeah. But I mean every hour." He pulled a black leather notebook from a pocket. "Look here."

"Got a system?"

"I always got a system. That's what they call me—Mickey System. But this one's a real barrel of brass. Maybe ten thousand systems I tried. But tonight I really hit it."

The guy was a tonic. His squeaky tones rambled on about his way of beating the dice and I just had to nod at intervals. He jumped up and down, chewed a stubby pencil. He lightened my mood a thousand per cent.

"See," he was saying. "I says to myself, Mickey, this is it. It's a mathematical certainty. A cinch. Seven you only make six ways, right? And if you take the odds without risking your line bet, the backline bet covers it, right? So you wind up with the house paying you to play. How about that?"

"How about that, indeed." I offered him a cigarette, got one for myself. "My name is Johnny Berlin."

"I know," he said and leaned forward for a light.

"You know?"

He nodded. "Along with everyone else in town. You got a reputation already."

"I'm hip. Someone tried to see if I could make a Ford fly Saturday night."

"Yeah." The laughter fled and I glimpsed a little steel in my companion. He glanced over his shoulder, back to me. "Funny things going on, Johnny. Walk easy." He straightened. "Speaking of walking, how's that for a strut?"

I turned. It was Gina. She really walked, that girl. Slim-legged, hips swinging. She was coolly poised as only a very beautiful woman can be. I hadn't seen half what this woman had to offer the other night. Her body was just on the verge of being too much. Ripe. Even lush. And she walked like a burlesque poser, all thrusting pelvis and steady shoulders. A clinging black jersey dress did its level best to hide the swelling lines, but only served to accentuate them. She walked right to me, took my hand.

"Johnny Berlin," she said. Her breasts were looking up and out. "How are you?"

"Ruined," I said. "Sit down. Have a drink."

I'd forgotten my crap-loving friend, naturally enough. Till his tie blinded me again. Evidently he and Gina were old friends. While they yakked, I ordered.

The drinks came and we had one apiece. Then Mickey took off for the game room to try his new system with larger markers. He'd checked it out with quarters. After he left we sat in silence for a while. Gina looked at her drink, fiddled with a lighter on the bar. Her perfume was dark and subtle, like crushed violets. The curve of her thigh touched my knee, left a blister.

"Gina," I said.

"Johnny Berlin." She turned. "How does one get a name like Johnny Berlin? It's so perfect for you."

"It's easy. You pick it yourself. At the orphanage they called me little Johnny Twenty-Two. I was the twenty-second foundling that year, or something. When I got big enough to care, I made one up for myself."

"Why Berlin?"

I shrugged. "It was easy to spell. I got it out of a newspaper when I ran off. I'd joined a carnival as a ride boy. They wanted a name. I gave 'em the first one I thought of. I've used it ever since. It's as good as any."

"I like it," she said. She pushed a coin around in the moisture. "Why did you call, Johnny?"

"Why did you come?"

She smiled, a flash of white between deep-red lips. She shook her hair and it was a midnight cloud.

"That's not fair. I suspect you're a cad, Johnny Berlin. I also suspect you know damn well why I came. This is a small town. There isn't much electricity."

"I guess we're both wired then." I leaned toward her, lowered my voice. "There is a feeling, Gina. You can call it anything you want to. But it's there. In the car the other night ..."

She put her hand on my arm, stopped me. "I know," she said. "Let's dance. This is much too public."

We danced. The floor wasn't crowded and we went very well together. She was tall and she danced like she walked, all thrusting pelvis and leggy glides. I was intensely aware of her body. My fingers tingled where I touched her.

Her hair brushed my face and I rubbed my chin in the black froth. She stirred.

"People are watching, Johnny. I have a husband, you know."

"Let 'em watch. Maybe they'll learn something."

She laughed, but her breath caught sharply. I kissed the tip of her ear, whirled her slowly and insinuatingly. She put her lips to my ear.

"No strings, Johnny? Just a ball, a few laughs? That's the way it has to be."

"No strings," I said. My throat was full of glue.

She pushed me away abruptly. "I'm loose as a wet Kleenex. Get me a drink. I'm going to the little girl's and repair my equanimity."

I held my arms wide in mock horror.

"I never touched it!"

Her full-throated laugh drifted over the music as she walked away. Her haunches slid under the jersey like firm chunks of Jello. I almost ran to the bar.

Waiting for the drinks I saw Jack Kilgallen with a slim redhead down the bar aways. A fat guy with silver hair wearing about three hundred dollars' worth of silk suit stood beside the pair. I figured him for Paul Carter. As I watched, the girl pulled away from Kilgallen, stumbled up the bar toward me. I heard her cussing the kid as she came.

She stopped in front of me, stood weaving on spike heels. She had a green sheath of satin, or something like it, on her almost hipless body; her legs were long and flashing in tan nylon.

"You're the guy," she said. "You're Johnny Berlin. You're big."

Everybody knew me. I turned, studied her.

"Back to your man, honey. No hassles tonight. I'm tied up."

"He says I'm drunk," she said. Her lipstick was smeared and the green, slightly sloe eyes focused reluctantly. A pretty kid. I've seen thousands like her in my racket. Fine, healthy girls pretending hardness and abandon to hide the memory of heartache.

"You think I'm drunk? I'm Sheila, Johnny Berlin."

I turned all the way on the stool. She slumped against me.

"Hey, easy. Stand up there. I'll buy you one drink. Then off you go. Okay?"

She nodded solemnly. I gestured for the bartender, cut my eyes down the bar to Kilgallen. He and Carter were in a heated argument. The kid looked like he wanted to come running. The drink came before he did and I handed it to Sheila. She promptly dropped it and reached for me. Warm lips found mine, clung. I had to hold her up or she'd have fallen. She twisted, let her hip rest on my thigh and kissed me very thoroughly indeed.

"I thought you were drunk," I said, drawing away from her.

"I'm not too drunk, honey." Her voice was brassy, loud in a sudden silence.

I looked up and saw Carter and the kid dealer surging up the length of the bar. Gina had come out of the back and stopped, an interested observer. All kinds of action. I pushed the girl upright.

"All right, baby. You've done the job. Get off it."

She stumbled erect, looked at me with a completely puzzled expression. But then Kilgallen and Carter arrived. I watched the rangy dealer closely. I wanted no more of those iron knuckles. I'd collected enough bruises in this town.

"Let her go, Berlin," the kid rasped.

"You're twisted, Kilgallen. She's holding me. And I don't like it. I think maybe you sent her. I think maybe someone wants me to be in trouble every time I turn around. I don't like that, either."

Carter pinned me with a level gambler's stare. His smooth face showed no emotion. He pulled the girl to him, quieted her. Kilgallen and I exchanged burning looks. The kid turned away, grabbed Sheila's arm.

"Come on," he said, jerking savagely at her.

"Jack! You're hurting me!"

Kilgallen wrenched the girl upright when she would have fallen, whacked her across the face with an open hand. I started from the stool. And Gina walked in front of me. I guess I looked pretty ridiculous. I sat back, watched Gina. My mind whizzed, hunting for something to say. She picked up her purse, lighter and cigarettes.

Carter said, "Berlin, I'd like to talk to you some time. Maybe we could make a deal. Donetti can't win, you know. You'd be wise to feather your nest elsewhere. We're not going to be pushed into syndication."

"Save it, Carter. I'm in the market for no deals. I run Dan Gurion's back room. Period. Got that?"

"That's all?"

"That's every damn bit. Except this—" I grabbed Gina's arm to keep her from leaving. "When I find out who wrecked my car I may expand my activities a little."

He nodded. Gina pulled at my hold.

"Please," she said. "I'd like to go home."

"Oh, now wait—"

Carter said, "Give my regards to your husband—Mrs. Donetti."

Gina stopped, looked at him coolly. "Tell him yourself, Paul. I don't carry messages. Or tell tales."

We got out of there. Gina had a black Buick tonight. I don't know what happened to the Cadillac. Maybe they had a stable. She got in, said nothing. The window was down.

I took a breath, the air moist and cool. Soon it would be foggy again.

I said, "It wasn't like that. You know that, don't you?"

"Please, Johnny. I'm tired."

"All right." I nodded. "Okay. Play it that way. But it won't work, baby. It flat won't work. And you know it."

She revved the engine to a snarl. For one split moment I saw something in the wide eyes—something dark and raw. Then it was gone. She pulled a scrap of handkerchief out of the cleft between her breasts, stuck it in my hand.

"Try that on your lips, darling."

The tires grated on rock and the car leaped into the darkness.

CHAPTER SIX

By the time I remembered my appointment with Ford Messner, I had a pretty fair glow on. Ordinarily I sip pretty easy around the funny water. It doesn't mix with gambling. But Gina's walk-out had left me with a high burn and I had to do something to dissipate it.

It was two-thirty and the Club Carroll was jumping. Thanks to our talent. Laddy Layton had evidently arrived early from Portland for his opening the next night at our joint. Anyhow, there he was on the bandstand, wringing sobs from one of his standards. The people were fractured. The creep was good.

I left the bar and went into the connecting room where Layton was killing the public. I saw Jack Kilgallen and the sultry Sheila, a more sober and considerably chastened Sheila, and Paul Carter.

Coley O'Rourke, my friend of earlier in the evening, had a table by himself. He seemed to be mentally murdering Kilgallen. At least his eyes stayed on the pair at the bar. On Sheila, really. I settled at a table by the outside door and looked around.

If Ford Messner were here yet I couldn't see him. It was just two thirty-five. I called a waitress and ordered. Across the room I spotted Condi, the Cherbourg's bartender, sitting with Bev and Dan.

The girl brought my drink and I dove into it. Layton's husky voice cut through the layers of smoke larded with glass tinkle and crowd murmur. It came to me that I'd spent too many of my nights in just such an atmosphere. A woman laughed shrilly. The later the hour the more shrill the laugh. I got a cigarette out, lit it, jerking savagely at the matches in the folder. Get off it, Berlin. The singer finished a number and the place erupted into sustained, enthusiastic applause. I slid down in my chair, stared at my cigarette end. Gina. What made her take the thing with Sheila so big? For that matter, who set the flaming redhead on me to begin with?

One thing had cleared up a little; whoever had nudged me into the canyon almost certainly had done so as a result of my arriving at the Cherbourg with Marino Donetti. I was beginning to understand why the little guy carried a gun. He wouldn't win any popularity awards around here. Which reminded me of his message. Call Donetti. I'd rather call Dr. Frankenstein.

"Could I sit here, please? The other tables are full."

I came out of my drink and met the bluest, clearest pair of eyes I'd seen in a long time. They belonged to a young girl standing opposite me. She was blonde, very cute, about eighteen or nineteen. Her skin was tan and firm and she wore a simple dress as if it had been made by Christian Dior.

I said, "Sure. Sit, kid. Be my guest."

She looked at me curiously, then slid into the chair across the table. I asked her if she wanted a drink, but she didn't hear me. She had her eyes riveted on Laddy Layton, sobbing on the bandstand about how far he'd walk for the girl he loved. I watched her. She sat twisted around in the chair, the firm body straining at attention, eyes glued to the slim, elegant figure of our entertainer. The curve of her cheek was a soft pink, like a ripe peach on a window sill with the afternoon sun carving it to brightness. There was something fresh about her. Clean, like hayrides and taffy-pulls and a thousand other things I'd only read about in my wandering existence.

Suddenly I felt old and weary. It wasn't often I doubted my own ability to shape my ends and make life what I wanted it to be. Except sometimes—like now—when a submerged something pulled at me, made me realize how little I really had.

The girl turned. "Isn't he the absolute most? He just does me up. I mean he's so way out."

"Oh, you bet," I muttered. I signaled a passing waitress. "You want a—well, a Coke or something?"

The girl nodded absently, attention once more on the singer. I ordered, looked around. Quite a crowd. Everyone who hadn't had his fill of lushing by the normal closing time for the other clubs had gravitated to the Carroll.

Way back in a corner a flash of platinum caught me familiarly and I half-stood to peer through the ever thickening haze of smoke. It was Fran. Looking like a hothouse orchid in all that din and reek. She wore white and her pale hair gleamed in the smoke like a pearl on black velvet. There was a man with her. All I could see were wide, solid-looking shoulders and a shock of brown hair. I waved, but she didn't see me.

I downed my drink, banged on the table with the empty glass. "Hey. Little service here."

My young companion turned.

"You," I said. "You're too damn young to be in a place like this. This late. Why don't you go home? Live a while before you start committing suicide."

Her young eyes sparkled in the subdued light. "You're crazy, Mr. Berlin. Just like Laddy said."

"You know me too." I looked away, a cold sensation creeping in me for no reason. "I'm getting used to it. Every place I go I'm a celebrity instead of a stranger. What the hell kind of a place is this?"

"Oh, you're notorious. Everyone is talking about the big war that might start between the gamblers now that you're here." She grinned, twisted on the chair. "Isn't it exciting? And Laddy works for you."

"What's with you and that jerk Layton?"

"Don't say that, Mr. Berlin." She frowned, then brightened. Layton had finished his turn and was making his way toward our table through the solid wall of applause. He'd made an impression here, all right. "Over here, Laddy," the girl called. She turned to me, whispered, "He came in the drugstore where I work early this evening. I was simply devastated. And when he asked me to meet him here, I almost died."

I grunted. The waitress came and left and Laddy Layton joined us at the table. That focused attention and everyone began waving at me. Layton greeted the girl like a returning Marine. Then he slid into a vacant chair, grinned at me.

"Hi, boss," he said. "I see you've met Carla—Carla Teacher. Isn't she a doll?"

"She will be when she grows up," I said.

Layton laughed. "He's a prude, honey. Hear him?"

Laddy was young and handsome in a slim, red-lipped, black-haired way. His chin was good and he wasn't skinny. He had an irritating way of seeming to look at the part in your hair when he talked.

Carla was too overcome to speak. Laddy put an arm around her, turned to me.

"You made a good deal, Berlin. When you hired me. I'll kill these yokels. They dig me, kid."

"That's what you're getting paid for. You want a drink?"

He ignored me, turned to the girl. His slim, manicured hand slid up the girl's bare arm, fingers working. He breathed audibly into her ear and she turned a bright crimson. Her eyes opened wide. Layton kissed her, tugged her dress away at the neck and ran a greedy tongue over the creamy skin of her neck. Carla shuddered and leaned against him. Her eyelids dropped and showed faintly luminous, her cherry lips sagged full and moist.

Layton said, "Umm, darling, you taste so good."

They acted like no one was within miles of them, mugging like mad. Layton kissed and fondled the kid, laughing and teasing her. He was having a ball; she was running into something she'd probably never experienced before.

"Hell of a show, huh?" a voice said.

Mickey System stood behind me. I was grateful for the interruption. In another minute I might have broken another cardinal Berlin rule—never butt into anybody's business for any reason whatever.

"How'd you do with the system?" I asked.

His shined cheeks sagged and he raised an eyebrow. "You know, it's a damn funny thing. I don't understand it. I had it made and all of a sudden, boom! I'm losing. Little by little."

A waitress came and we ordered. I was getting warm again, my belly unknotting and the smoky blue rising in my head. It felt good. Better than thinking.

"Listen," Mickey said. The eyes were dark now, hard. "I don't know what's going on, but I've felt a couple of rumbles tonight. Something's in the air. And you seem to be right in the middle of it."

"What the hell for?"

He shook his head. "Look, Carter and O'Rourke have been feuding for years. Now I understand they've set up a meeting of all of the operators for day after tomorrow. Including Dan Gurion. I don't know whether he knows it yet or not. It's just a rumble, like I said. But you be careful. A lot of people are edgy. And when people are edgy, things happen."

"Like what? What're you trying to say, Mickey?"

"I've said it, man."

He leaned back, turned on the grin. But it didn't fool me anymore. This guy had a hard core. I recognized it, having spent most of my life with people just like him. Good hustlers look like rubes and when one as rubbish as Mickey System comes along, look out.

He got up and left before I could figure out what to say to him. Everyone talked about an Association, but nobody knew anything about it. I decided I'd have no peace until I had it all straight. Only one way to do that—go see Donetti. When I'd resolved to see him the next day I felt better. I could even watch Layton corrupt the eager young soda clerk without losing the supper I hadn't eaten.

"Hi, Johnny." Bev ran a hand around my neck.

"Hello, doll. Everything all right?"

She shrugged. "Dan's real happy with you. But he's suspicious. I tried to tell him you didn't have anything to do with Donetti."

"I don't care what he thinks."

"You loaded, Johnny?"

I grinned up at her. She put her lips close to my ear. "What's with this bit?" Her eyes fastened on Layton and Carla. They'd gotten to where the girl's dress had been pulled away far enough to expose one swelling, young breast almost entirely. "If you're the chaperone, you're doing a lousy job."

"None of my business," I said. I got up, steadied myself. Layton looked up. "Powder my nose," I said to him. "Why don't you take the kid home?"

His eyes, moist and shining, narrowed. "Why don't you mind your own business, Berlin?"

I shrugged, got away from there. Dan Gurion high-balled me as I passed his table, but I kept going. I ran cold water over my wrists, washed my face. The cold water helped. Then I combed my hair, taking plenty of time. If Messner wanted to see me badly enough, he'd wait. When I got back to the main room, the chilly dealer still hadn't shown and my table was empty.

The girl Carla was gone. I missed her. Like I'd lost a ten-dollar bill I wasn't sure I'd had in the first place. Layton was singing again. He winked at me from the stand. I sat, got a Camel going.

And the building shook.

Layton trailed off flatly. The buzz of conversation and the noises from the crap table in the back room stopped abruptly, like someone had pulled a switch. When the wrenching jar shuddered through the room the rafters sifted dust and all movement ceased. A car horn began to blow outside. For just an instant there was no sound at all except the mournful, sustained blast of the auto horn.

I was closest to the door and I went out of it like a bookie in a vice raid. Nobody got out before me. The bar entrance was on the other side of the building. I didn't think of it then, but later it became important and I'm damned sure I went through that door before anyone else did.

I noticed the fog. I noticed the chill that had crept from the sea and the wet asphalt stretching past the club on two sides. I could even smell the clay of the parking area. Then I saw the car.

A green Cadillac, its nose crumpled against the frame building, a man hanging half out of the window on the driver's side. Carla stood beside the car, her mouth crammed full of shaking fingers. For just a moment it didn't register. I saw the man. I saw Carla. The scene was lewdly illuminated by the stripping of red neon running around the eaves of the building. Then I saw the blood.

Marino Donetti lay slumped over the sill of the Cad's window, clutching a gun in one small hand. His neck was a mess of blood and he looked like a man overdue for dying. I jumped off the porch, ran to the car. The little man had a look of fierce concentration on his face. His lips moved. The girl stood frozen. I saw that half of Donetti's neck had been shot away. He should have been dead.

As I reached the car he twisted in the window, made a supreme effort to speak. I caught a sibilant flow of words before a gout of blood rushed over his lips, splattered the shining door. He was dead, slumped against the wheel. The horn blasted and continued to blow.

One arm hung from the window, the gun still clutched. Dark blood dripped from the knuckles to the wet clay of the parking lot. The girl began to scream.

Somebody behind me said, "Holy Christ!" over the sound of the car horn.

I reached for the wailing girl, slapped her sharply. She stopped screaming, began crying with her mouth wide open to the foggy night. I shot a glance over my shoulder while holding the girl against me. Mickey System jumped from the porch, came at a run. Beside him, Ford Messner, for once shaken out of his deadly calm, strode. His white eyebrows twisted to match the creases in his cheeks at the sight of the dark head lolling messily over the car window.

Mickey said, "Donetti! For Chrissake!"

I took one arm from the girl, spun the little dice hustler. "Call somebody, Mickey. Everybody. Meat wagon, fuzz. And hurry."

Then the people boiled out of the building and everything got all mixed up. A woman began wailing, higher than the horn sound and someone slapped her too. I pulled Carla away from the car, tried to comfort her. Messner stuck right with me. Somebody reached in the car, pulled Donetti off the horn button.

The quiet was like a blow.

I said, "Ford, you hear what this guy said before he checked out?"

The man looked at me for a moment without speaking. His face had regained its accustomed blankness; the eyes looked like two pearl onions in a white crème de menthe frappe.

"What he said?"

"Yes, what Donetti said. Just before he died I thought he said something. But I didn't catch what it was. Did you?"

He shook his head. "I came out behind Mickey. Ask him."

I looked at him. "It's not important."

The girl in my arms tried to get away. I held her, patted her head. She looked up at me and never have I seen such stark and absolute fear in a human expression. Her eyes were wild and rolling.

"Let me go, let me go!" she whispered. "Please let me go."

Dry sobs racked her. I could feel every tense line of her. The sobs were wrenching and powerful, like getting hit in the belly with a pool cue.

"Easy, honey. Nobody's going to hurt you. I promise. Tell me something, Carla. Did you hear Donetti say anything?"

She tried to break away from me again. Now she was crying in earnest.

"Carla!" I shook her. "Did you hear what he said? You were closer than I was. You must have heard."

"No! I didn't hear anything! Nothing. Oh, nothing!"

She pulled away, looked at me as if she didn't know who I could possibly be. I tried to hold her, but she swallowed a sob and tore herself out of my encircling arms with a furious burst of strength. A hand gripped my arm when I would have followed. She ran around the building toward the rear of the club, the red light dying her tanned legs and honey hair to a blood red.

Messner had my arm. He let go when I spun around. "Let her go," he said. "She's shook. Let her wipe her eyes or something."

"But I wanted to find out—"

"You're no cop," the dealer said. He jerked his chin toward the door. "This guy'll take care of what has to be done. You better get a story ready yourself."

An authoritative voice began steadying the crowd. It was the big gun who'd been with Fran Cole. He pushed people right and left, striding toward the car and the still-settling corpse.

"All right, everybody." His voice was big as he was. Broad and sun-burned and very competent looking. "Let's get together on this."

The rumble died a little. The big man stopped beside me, spared me a piercing glance, then turned back to the crowd.

"God damn it, I said everybody!" he yelled. "Get the hell back inside! All of you."

I didn't move. Neither did Messner. But the others began drifting back into the club, craning necks, morbidly curious at

PHILIP RACE

the same time they were repelled by the sight. Inside someone dropped a coin in the juke and ribald sound blasted out into the gray night.

"Everybody," the big man said, pushing Condi Capucho with a huge hand. "You all know me. I'm in charge till the Chief gets here."

Fran Cole broke away from the crowd at the door, ran toward me. Her eyes were wide and frightened and she ran with long strides, like a boy. At each step her thigh threatened to tear the white skirt. She got almost to me, stopped abruptly.

"Johnny. Johnny, did you see—"

"Easy, honey." I put out a hand. "What's the rush? You go back in and take care of that little kid, that Carla. She's scared blue."

The girl's eyes ran over my face, skipping, searching. She pulled me away from the car, the ugly sight of Donetti still leaning out the window.

"Johnny, did you—" She stopped, bit her full underlip. "What I mean is—Oh, Christ! I don't know what I mean. Tell me something, damn it!"

I grinned at her. A little sick, but a grin. "I didn't kill him, honey. What for?"

"Good." Her eyes dropped and suddenly she seemed to realize she was standing very close to me. I liked it. But she moved back. "I got caught inside. Someone said Donetti was ... dead. And that you were there. I—"

The big guy was still trying to get things under control. He had Mickey System and one of the dealers from the club helping him herd the curious.

"Inside, inside." His big voice was sharp in the chill night. "Harley, you watch the back. Nobody goes out at all. Got that?"

"Means us too, I guess," I said.

She nodded.

50

"Just a minute, Berlin."

The big guy was talking to me. Fran must have told him my name. But then everybody in the God-damn state knew my name. I pulled away from the girl, started toward him.

"Johnny," Fran said, walking with me, "this is George French. An old friend. He's—"

"Detective-Lieutenant George French," he said. The red neon accentuated the high color of his face. He was broad all over, this guy; he had thick brown hair growing far down over his forehead. "I've been hearing quite a bit about a guy named Berlin lately. Now you find a body. Me and you should talk, I think. What do you think?"

"I think—"

"I don't care what you think," he said. He looked at Fran a long time, then at me. She stood there, shivering slightly in the thin dress, her fine face haloed by the mist and the reflected light. Finally he growled, "Get over there by the building. I'll get to you. You," he said to Fran, "get inside."

"George, I want to explain about—"

"Get inside, Fran," he said.

French didn't get to me until after the rest of the cops arrived. They sirened into the lot, slid to slewing halts among the parked cars. Orders crackled. Blue coats and white coats ran here and there; flash bulbs smoked and popped. Just like the big time. I stood against the wall and smoked one cigarette after another. There was a watery, loose feeling in my stomach.

The lieutenant barked orders to cover exits, photograph and dust the murder car, get names and pre-check alibis. He knew his business. He detailed a bunch of harness bulls to beat the bushes in an ever-widening perimeter till they found the spot where the shooting had occurred. It was obvious even to me that Donetti hadn't been shot in the parking lot. And that he hadn't driven far with a hole the size of a pencil in one of the main veins of his neck.

"Find the marks of a car, walk careful. Real careful. Look for footprints. It's muddy so you'll find some." He turned to me. "What size shoe you wear, hard guy?"

"Ten," I said. "But—"

French was roaring after the departing squad. "Ten, the man says. First clubfoot ruins a print I'll personally guarantee he walks the docks till his ass barnacles!"

He turned to me with a hard smile that had nothing to do with his narrowed eyes. He grabbed my arm, steered me toward a police car standing there with its red light glowing.

"Tell me something, slicker," he said tightly. "Talk and just keep talking till you get me out of the notion I'm in right now."

CHAPTER SEVEN

W e talked in the police car, me in the front seat and Lieutenant
French sharing the other with a little black notebook. Or
rather I talked. He contributed occasional grunts and wry snorts.
He began by operating on the premise that I was an out-of-town
hooligan sent by the syndicate to wipe out Donetti. I finally got
him talked out of that.

I'd been hard-pressed to explain my motives to him. Why,
after coming on the town by accident in the fog, hadn't I just kept
on going? And further, why was I traveling in the first place? A
cop is eternally a cop. It isn't nearly enough that you tell them
what, they always want to know why. And sometimes a guy
just doesn't know why. Could I tell him a leggy redhead named
Charlene had made it uncomfortable for me in Nevada and I'd
left rather than hassle with her? Could I tell him about the ugly
streak born early into little Johnny Twenty-Two at the orphanage—the hard necessity to get back at whomever harmed him
or threatened to? No, of course I couldn't. Any more than I had
ever been able to discuss those things, the chaff of an early life I'd
been running for years to forget.

"You left the room," French said. His wide eyes lifted from
the book on his knee. "You said you went to the—what'd you
call it?"

"The doniker. But look, Lieutenant—"

"Men's room," the lieutenant said and shrugged. "Okay.
What time was it? When you made your trip?"

I said, "It must have been about ten minutes or so before the Cad hit the building. But I was inside when that happened. Anyone can tell you. I just got sick of seeing that Layton mess with this young kid, see, and I got up before I stuck my nose where it didn't belong. So I went to the don—men's room. When I got back, they'd gone. I sat there a while, not very long. And then boom! The joint began to shake."

French grunted. "All right, tell me again."

"Everything, for Christ's sake?"

He stuck a crumpled butt in his slash of a mouth, fired it with my lighter and shook his head.

"Just the part about what you saw when you came out the door. And what you thought Donetti said."

I sighed and reached over the seat back for one of my cigarettes. I got it lit, and settled in the front seat, sitting crossways, one leg drawn up on the seat.

"It's funny. I can close my eyes right now and see it all again. Like it was suspended in my memory, frozen there. I jumped out the door as soon as the car hit. The mist had just begun to settle and the spotlights on the poles had the parking area pretty well lit. And the neon around the roof. I remember thinking what a pattern the combination of light made on the kid's dress, on her face. That's what I saw first, the kid. Carla. She was standing there right by the Cad's front fender, both hands up to her face. Her eyes were as big as five-dollar chips."

I stopped for a minute, reliving the scene. It was very quiet. The cops had got everyone back inside the building; the basket wagon had been and gone. Only the scratch of French's old-fashioned pen and the buzz of neon disturbed the fog-held tranquility of the Oregon night.

"Then I saw the car," I said. I sucked on the cigarette. It tasted like the stuff janitors use to sweep the floor. I pushed open the windwing, flipped it out. "Pretty well smashed up. The hood had slammed up when the car hit, I guess. Anyway, the nose was crumpled and this guy was hanging out the window. He was still alive."

"You knew who it was right away?"

I thought about it. Then I nodded. "Yeah. I guess I did. But it must have been because of the car. I only met him once for a few minutes so I wouldn't know him like a brother. But I'm sure I knew right away it was Donetti. Besides all night people have been accusing me of working for him, working against him. Everything but being his father."

French grunted. His eyes, shadowed by the shelf of hard bone above them, came up from the notebook.

"Which way is it?"

"You too, huh?" I twisted on the seat. "You want to hear the rest of the story?"

"Why don't you want to talk about it? Were you working with Donetti? Did somebody send you here to enlarge the syndicate operations?"

"Lieutenant, I'm tired of talking about it. I don't belong to anybody. I'm Johnny Berlin and if you'd spend a quarter on a wire to Reno you could find it out. If the county hasn't got the dough I'll pick up the tab myself. But I'm sick of having every damn joker ask me questions I haven't got any answers for. Now if you want to talk about what happened tonight, let's get with it. Anything else, book me and I'll call a lawyer."

"Like that, huh?"

"Just like that, friend. I'm cooperative. I got no big record—don't want one. But nobody shoves me around. That includes cops."

For a minute I thought he was going to make me prove it. The hard planes of his face sharpened in the pink shadow and he seemed to edge forward on the seat. After a moment he was all business again.

"Go on from seeing the car," he said.

"Like I told you, I saw the little girl first. I thought maybe she came out to wrestle with that singer in somebody's back seat. But then I saw Donetti and I ran to the Cadillac. He was trying to say something. Trying hard. His throat was a mess and he kept looking at the girl, his lips forming words that his throat just didn't have the wind for."

I stopped, turned to the window for a minute. The scene was still fresh; the sight of the greasy blood rolling sluggishly down the green door still behind my eyes.

French said softly, "Okay, Berlin. It was bad. What did Donetti say?"

"He said to get Johnny Ronns. Or Blounce. Something like that and that's the best I can do. I told you. The guy was dying, should have been dead. And I wasn't listening too closely either, if you want to know. The first name was Johnny. I'm sure of that. The last could have been anything like that. Ronns, Ronce—maybe even Brown, I don't know. But I told you before the girl was right there—right by the fender. The car must have damn near hit her. If I heard a little, she heard a lot."

The lieutenant sighed. He closed the book, slapped it on Ms thigh.

"Okay, Berlin. Don't leave town. If you find out anything, let me know. This ain't Reno. It's McKaneville. And I'm the law. Don't forget it. I'll take care of the girl. You better watch your back for a while."

"What do you mean by that?"

He shrugged. "Lot of people pulling in different directions in this thing. All of them, for one reason or another, seem to think you have something to do with it. I'd be careful if I were you."

"Can I have my stuff?"

He handed me the junk they'd taken in the pre-questioning shakedown. All but one item. The little knife. He looked at it, tossed it up and caught it. His slate eyes bore into mine.

"This too, slicker," he said. His voice was very soft. "Take your toy. And be careful with it. Next time you cut someone it may be a citizen somebody cares about."

I took it. The blade was crusted with blood.

Feet crunched on wet clay and a young policeman, wide in the shoulder and very scrubbed and eager looking, walked to the car. He tapped the window. French rolled it down.

"What is it, Tommy?"

"Got Mrs. Donetti, Lieutenant," he said. "Took her downtown, got a positive I.D."

I turned on the seat and wiped moisture off the window so I could see out. Gina was just walking away from a police sedan, walking with that challenging stride, head held high, hair streaming. I couldn't see her face, but I'd bet she wouldn't cry.

French told the kid he'd be right in, to hold Mrs. Donetti. Then he turned back to me.

"That's all, Berlin," he said. His voice was flat, without hint of feeling.

"Look, French. I don't know what you're trying to do here, but I can damn well prove I was inside when the car hit the building. Now granted that—is there any way in hell you can tab me for this push?"

He studied me before answering. Then he shook his head back and forth. "Granting that," he said. "But you left the table."

"To go to the doniker, for Chrissake!"

He opened the car door, stepped out into the parking lot. I climbed out, stretched automatically. French slammed the door, stood with his big hand on the wet metal.

"The doniker, as you put it, has a window, slicker." His jaw jutted suddenly and he took a half step toward me. "I'd like to prove you climbed out of it."

Inside, I shrugged away from all the questions and moved back into the main room, looked around. It was a hushed crowd. And the room was getting smelly what with smoke and dying perfume and wet cloth. Messner and Laddy Leyton shared a table with Carla. The youngster looked a little calmer now. And Sheila.

The smoldering redhead tossed her curls at me and smiled. She had lipstick on her teeth.

I saw Dan and Bev at a table in the rear. Dan looked haggard. I suddenly remembered that we had a grand opening that night and neither of us had been to bed for something like a long twenty-four. He waved and I pushed through the bored, sleepy, still-frightened throng and set the steaming cup of coffee I had picked up in the kitchen on the table.

"Hi," Bev said wearily.

"We open tonight," Dan said. "New policy. Fine entertainment." He pushed a hand through his hair, blew out his breath.

"Take it easy," I said. "This won't figure. Might help business with Layton here and all. Bunch of reporters around. They'll splash it in the local rags. Which reminds me, don't forget to take that quarter page in the daily paper like I told you."

"Okay, Johnny." He straightened, looked at my coffee. "Wonder if we can get some of that?"

I got a waitress. She was tired and very irritable, but I talked her into bringing coffee. For a while nobody said anything. Then Dan asked the question I'd been waiting for.

"Johnny ... did French accuse you of being—well, of working with Donetti?"

I sipped my coffee, cursed when it burned my tongue.

"Yes, Dan. He accused me. Does everybody think I'm a syndicate hoodlum, for Christ sake. You too?"

He hunched his big shoulders, leaned over the table. "Look, Johnny. I like you. You know that. But there has to be some reason for all this sudden heat. I don't pretend to be well enough informed to know where it's coming from. And you, well, you did arrive just when the pressure began to mount."

"And with Donetti," I added. "Don't forget that."

"All right," he said. "With Donetti. What does French think? You and I can fight some other time."

I nodded. "French thinks the little guy got it because he had been exerting pressure on the owners—that's you and O'Rourke and Carter and the rest—to get together in some sort of bloc. And he thinks Donetti was backed by out-of-town money. Maybe out-of-town muscle."

"What kind of backing?" Dan asked, looking up from his coffee "Organized? Or just some of his hoodlum friends from San Francisco?"

The question was too sharply asked. My friend and boss was digging in a new direction; his eyes had hardened, grown opaque. I wasted a minute lighting a smoke, let the question hang there.

Finally I said, "What're you trying to say, Dan? For one time let's lay it all out, huh? I'm getting tired of having people playing me for a jerk. And if we're going to work together—if you want to go ahead with the opening tonight—we'd better work a better basis of mutual trust than we have so far."

Dan bit his lip and considered the table intently. He looked like a two-dollar better with only one ninety-eight.

"Johnny, when you asked me the other day if anyone knew whether Donetti had his own money in the Play Spot, I told you I didn't know. That's not true. I do know. At the time I—"

"All right. Never mind the rehash. Go on with the tale."

He nodded. "Several of us decided a long time ago that the Devil's Lake property was beyond a man like Donetti. For business reasons we decided we should know what we were up against." The horn-rimmed glasses flashed from his pocket and he polished the lenses vigorously. The heavy jaw tightened as he talked. "We found out who was backing it. Rory Boise, the district attorney, helped us with it. We were naturally afraid of a concentrated influx of new money. Especially syndicate money. So we checked."

"How?"

Dan set his cup down, rubbed his eyes. "Private detective. We hired a good Portland agency. The reports came quickly, all authenticated. Donetti was—I think the words were percentage manager. A front organization floated the issue on a huge cash transfer to an operational account for the Devil's Lake Development Company. An outfit called Gilbertson Enterprises, Incorporated uttered the letter of transfer. The agency we hired didn't know that this outfit was a syndicate operation. That information came to us confidentially from Rory Boise."

I didn't say anything. I didn't like this at all. I didn't like thinking about what would happen to whomever had pushed the little gambler. Not at all. Dan slipped his coffee, pushed back in the chair.

"So," he said, exhaling, "you see why we were worried, are still worried. That's why we set up meetings, argued, fought. We knew this territory was potentially a million-dollar setup if it could be exploited correctly. When Donetti came on with his Gambler's Protective Association, we backed off quick. It smelled to us like the first step. Now it looks like we might have been right."

I said, "You were right. But it won't do you any good."

"What do you mean?"

"Who do you think killed him?"

He blinked, startled. "I hadn't thought ..."

"He didn't plink himself in the jugular, friend. Somebody set him up for a meeting. Probably close to the Carroll here. Somebody he knew. And somebody he trusted."

"How can you know that?"

I grinned a little. "I know," I said. "And if it was done close—and it had to be—then somebody in this room right now did it."

That stopped conversation. Dan studied his coffee. I watched Layton and Carla. The singer wasn't charming her now. She sat there like a hard-rubber statue, not answering questions or offering anything to the talk at the table. After a while I turned away. Finally I got up and walked out.

Dawn had come. It would be a good one. A red sun hung over the timbered mountains to the east, burning away the haze. Tops of cars glinted wetly. The canvas-shrouded shape of the green Cadillac sat still crumpled against the wall of the club. I took a breath, chased the smoke and perfume from my lungs. The air was sharp, morning clear; trees and water, mountains and mist.

She stepped out onto the small porch beside me. I didn't turn, she didn't speak for a moment. We watched the clearing morning sky together. The scent, that maddening hint of crushed violets, came to me. It was suddenly very quiet.

I said, "Hello, Gina," without turning.

"Hello, Johnny."

"Rough on you, kid."

"When you play with fire I guess you get burned, Johnny." She said it clearly, without emotion. I don't know what I expected. Some phony collection of worn phrases, sorrowful and meaningless. I lifted my head.

"Smell that sea air?"

"The lake is beautiful in the morning, Johnny. The trees are reflected in the water and all the funny little waves flash the sun around." Her voice deepened. "You should see it."

I turned then, gripped her upper arms. Her eyes were wide and clear. The mass of hair was unbound and blowing free, blacker than a gambler's heart.

"What are you trying to say, Gina?"

She glanced quickly at the closed door of the club, then moved frankly against me. Her lips touched my chin.

"I made a mistake last night, running off. I don't want to make the same one again ..."

CHAPTER EIGHT

I fastened my gaze to the tiny gold pin, a crouching leopard, on the collar of Gina's suit. She was stiff against me, waiting for my reaction to her words.

"They got you out of bed, I guess."

She nodded.

"But then you got to bed real early."

She pulled away, her lids dropping. "Yes," she said. "Very early. I'm trying to apologize for that, Johnny. You're not making it easy."

I spun away, walked to the edge of the small porch.

"Don't you care who killed your old man?"

She followed me. I didn't turn, but I could feel the magnetic force of her. I closed my eyes and I could see that impossible body, those pouting lips.

"Johnny. Johnny, listen. Marino and I—well, we've been nothing to each other for a long time. A very long time. I guess if you made me be honest I'd have to say no, I don't care who killed him. Or why. He was a grown man, capable of doing his own thinking. You want me to be a hypocrite? You want me to be dewy-eyed? Well, I'm sorry. I'm not like that and I won't pretend."

I turned. "Okay. Let it be like that, then."

"Like that, then," she said. Then, "Johnny, listen. It's got to be better than that. Remember the electricity? Remember the certainty we both had? Why should we let Donetti ruin it, spoil our discovery of each other? He's dead. It's finished for him and nothing we do can hurt or help him. He's through and we're alive." She touched me lightly with her fingertips, brushing them over my face. "It was ended for me a long while ago, darling. Last night he wouldn't have mattered to you, would he?"

I took a breath, shook my head. A head popped out of the door, withdrew again. The young cop, checking on us.

"Then why should he matter now?"

Her eyes searched mine. For a moment the caress in them, the bold invitation bothered me. I thought of Fran Cole and her cool beauty, her almost prim façade. Then I shook the feeling. This was my kind of woman. Warm and willing, alive and available; not withdrawn behind fluttering handkerchiefs; not a statue of purity to stand back from and admire with your mouth hung open.

"French is through with you, isn't he?" I asked.

"Yes, Johnny. He's satisfied. I told him Marino left Devil's Lake about midnight. I didn't see him again until—"

She broke off, turned away. I pulled her around roughly, lifted her chin with a finger. Her eyes were closed; deep blue traced the hollows. A pulse stirred at the side of her throat, pushed the skin outward with its movement. I covered the ripe lips with mine, felt them open. The crushed violets drifted up, mixed with woman-scent. Her arms started around my neck and I stopped them, gripped the slim wrists.

"No," I said, pulling my lips away. "Get in that Ford over there." I pointed to my rented heap. "I'll clear it with French. Go. Go on."

She wet her lips, nodded. For a moment she dropped her forehead to my chest. Then she twisted away, ran down the steps.

I went through the door into the club. The crowd was getting restless now. A solid murmur had built up in the room, querulous and irritable. I saw French by the bandstand and set a course through the tables toward him. He had Ford Messner backed up against the stand, questioning him. A police stenographer flanked him. The dealer's funny white eyebrows were mussed, but his face was controlled as always. His glance found me, held briefly.

French said, "You didn't hear Donetti say anything? Call a name, maybe?"

"No." Ford turned slowly to me as I got to the small group, stopped. His eyes were cold, his face expressionless. "And as far as I know, no one heard him say anything. The Teacher kid, Carla, was right by the car. She says she didn't hear anything."

French slipped his own notebook into his pocket and gestured dismissal to the stenographer. "At least," he rasped, "she says she didn't."

The lieutenant stretched, widening the broad shoulders. His red face was all angles and planes in the harsh interior light. He saw me and nodded sourly, shook his head a trifle.

"Yeah, I heard it," I said. "Somebody's lying like a dog." I looked at Messner. "Ain't that right, chilly? Wouldn't you say someone was fibbing?"

Messner said nothing. I turned back to French.

"Where is the kid, Lieutenant?"

"Sent her home. With Fran. Couldn't get anything out of her." He shot a look at Messner. "Except that she hadn't heard anything. How do you account for that, slicker?"

I said, "That's a good question. Maybe you should lean on this icicle here. He shoots a pretty fair stick in that lie department."

Messner stiffened. "What do you mean, Berlin?"

"You know what I mean. If you came out behind me like you said, then you heard the man say something. Or try to. Because I damn sure did."

"You say."

"That's right, chilly. I say."

I tried to step around French; the big cop blocked the move with a shoulder.

"No," he said. "None of that."

Messner turned away.

I said, "Lieutenant, I'm taking Mrs. Donetti back to Devil's Lake. You can forget the car for her."

French looked at me for a long moment. His slab-featured face reflected none of his thoughts. The cop finally nodded, brushed me aside and bellowed for attention. He was sending everyone home. The weary crowd stirred and began moving. Messner started by me, turning sideways in the cramped space between the bandstand and the adjacent table. I touched his arm.

"You forget our appointment?"

He looked at me. He stood poised and neat in his brown suit, maroon shirt; he clutched a tan leather attaché case in one hand. Messner was one of those fortunate guys who never wrinkle a suit. After the long night, the wilting events just past, he still looked fresh and natty. His white eyebrows raised at my question and one corner of his mouth quirked just a little.

"Let's say it's called because of wet grounds."

I stepped close to him. His eyes narrowed and one hand closed into a fist.

"Listen, Messner. I'm not connected in any way with this local hassle. Got that? I don't know from syndicates and I never met Donetti in my life before Saturday night. Now you get that. And you pass it around. Because from now on I'm going to be as touchy as a sun-burned chorus girl. It would be a whole lot better if everyone left me alone."

I turned and started off.

"Berlin."

I stopped. He hadn't changed position or expression.

"You got lucky last night at Coley's," he said, thin lips barely moving. "Don't push that luck too far."

Then he was gone. He drifted into the crowd eddying around the main door before I could get my jaw unhinged.

Gina was waiting in the Ford. She sat staring blankly at the wall of the club, one arm out the window, a forgotten cigarette burning in her slim fingers.

"Any trouble?"

"No," I said. "No trouble."

I slid into the Ford, got it started and we got out of there. I drove fast, pouring the Ford around the twisting road as fast as it would take the curves. I watched the flashing, morning-wet asphalt and worked out some of my resentment through the vibrant steering wheel, the squealing tires. Gina just sat, head thrown back to the breeze.

She laughed out loud and I spared a glance from the rushing road. Gina had her face in the rush of air from the windwing, laughing in the cool surge. The black hair streamed and whipped across her face.

"Johnny," she called, still laughing. "Johnny, we're alive and it's summer!"

"You're crazy."

The Ford nosed over the small rise and there was Devil's Lake, bluer than blue, nestled in the timbered shoulders of surrounding mountains. There was a long, narrow pier and some boats and a swimming float out from a white beach, bobbing slightly in the sapphire swell.

The Devil's Play Spot lay in the slight depression. It was quite a layout. I'd been prepared for a pretty smooth operation since Gurion's description. A crushed rock drive bellied out in a circle from the entrance road. The casino sat facing us as we drove slowly down into the declivity. It was a symphony in sea-foam candy sprinkled with diamonds. Glass and neon and creamy stucco. Atop the main building, a huge figure of a red-caped, horned and tailed devil crouched. Streaks of neon, flames when they were lit, surrounded the figure. Spotted around the driveway that went around the hotel were cottages and bungalows of pink stucco with red-tiled roofs; all alike and all gleaming in the early sun. The front of the casino was glass and white marble, the entrance to the lobby flanked by stacked pillars of fieldstone.

Gina motioned me around to the right as I slowed approaching the parking lot at the side of the hotel-casino. Not one single sign of life disturbed the modern exactness of the décor. Lights showed from the lobby's gloom; undoubtedly someone was on duty within.

"That cabana all the way down on the right," she said. "The blue one."

"All the rest are pink," I said, wheeling the Ford in accordance with her instructions.

"Darling, you're a brilliant conversationalist."

I grinned. "I been sick."

She pushed against me, bit lightly at my neck and murmured something. I got the car into the carport anyhow. The blue cottage was right on the water, the last in the line. A little larger and a little smarter than the rest.

It was quiet. A bird cried somewhere and the waves lapped the shore softly.

"Doesn't seem to be much activity."

Gina stirred against me. She raised her head, blinked at the swaying water.

"It's eight in the morning, Johnny."

"Yeah, but this is a resort. Isn't it?"

She laughed deep in her throat. She twisted on the seat, back to the steering wheel, fell across me. Her arms slid around my neck.

"It's not that kind of a resort, darling."

She framed my face with her hands, looking into my eyes. Hers were dark and all pupil, half-shrouded by drooping lids. A pink tongue came out, ran slowly over the purple pads of her lips. I pulled her roughly against me, bending to meet her mouth.

"Don't be a caveman, Johnny," she said against my lips. "Slowly, darling. Slowly. We have all the time in the world."

"Not too much of this," I said. "I can't stand too damn much of this."

She nuzzled for a moment, then pulled away abruptly. The wild black of her hair spilled streaks of light from the sun's fingers.

"Well, look at us," she said. Her breasts rose up and down with her rapid breathing. "Your hand is warm, darling."

"Gina..."

She kissed me quickly.

"Say it again."

"Say what?"

"My name." She leaned back, dropped her lids. "Just say my name, Johnny."

I freed my hand, slid it under her upper arm and held her away from the steering wheel. Her fingers traced my face, my lips fondled her ear.

"Gina," I said, making it a promise.

She closed her eyes, pulled against me suddenly. She lay against me. Her lashes brushed my neck. My fingers tingled wherever I touched her.

"How about the car? Is it wise to leave it right out in plain sight?"

Gina pulled away, slid off my lap. Her hands worked at the wild tangle of black hair.

"The hell with the car," she said. Her nostrils were flattened; the black skirt had climbed to mid-thigh.

She pushed open the door, slid her legs out, then turned to look at me. "Coming?"

There must have been a front room to the bungalow, but I didn't see it. I didn't see much of anything except the swirling pink dots and the figure of Gina striding ahead with her curious glide. Her hands tore at her clothing and by the time we got to the bedroom, she was down to wispy under-things, holding her skirt in her hand.

"You going to pull the curtains?" I asked.

She threw the skirt on a chair, kicked off her shoes. Then she came to me, posed with one hand on her hip.

"Don't you want to see what you're getting?"

"Oh, for Christ's sake, don't be coy. I was thinking about you. I don't give a damn."

"Then don't worry about me, darling. Just be good to me."

I grabbed her and she stopped me with a whispered, "Wait."

"What now?"

She turned. "Unfasten me, Johnny."

Somehow we got to the bed and the waves outside the window kicked reflections into the room, speckling the walls and ceiling.

She said my name over and over and I didn't say anything at all. I couldn't have said anything, even for the deed to Las Vegas. And oddly, in the midst of my fatigue and passion and the overpowering excitement of the woman in my arms, I thought of Fran Cole. Cool Fran. Blonde and tight and poised no end.

"Your hands, Johnny," Gina said through her teeth. "Oh, I love your hands!"

She whimpered and pressed against me and blood rushed through my veins like tiny knives cutting me off from life for one pulsing instant.

CHAPTER NINE

A faint shout drifted in from one of the bathers on the beach; a motor boat chattered on the lake. The late afternoon sun flooded the cheerful, yellow-and-silver room, made the rumpled bed cozy.

I stared at the ceiling. "Gotta go."

Gina moved her leg, let the warm length of it touch me. "You sure?"

"Yeah. I'm sure. You're a doll and I dig you, but I promised Dan I'd be there early tonight. The opening bit, you know?"

She nodded, said nothing. I liked it. Just lying there, rested from the few hours' sleep, sated from a memorable experience. Nothing sloppy, nothing sticky. Just a ball; a healthy, uncomplicated woman, a lot of fun and nobody hurt. Not like it would be with Fran Cole. That would be a production. If you ever managed to get her into bed. Tears and protestations of undying I'll-never-forget-you love, with messy indecision and foolish fumbling. Not for me, not for Johnny Berlin.

"Johnny. You know anybody in Frisco? Any of the big gamblers?"

"Huh? What kind of question is that?"

"Well, you came from that direction. You're a dealer. I figured you'd know some of 'em, maybe could give me a line I could use when I leave here."

"When you leave? What's the angle? You got a pretty good deal here, seems to me. Or was that just Donetti?"

She nodded. "Marino. He never told me anything. I had nothing to do with the business."

"How about the—I mean I heard about a high-class…" I didn't know how to put it so I stopped.

"The girls?"

"Yeah, all right. The girls."

She shrugged, handed her stub of cigarette to me. "We got 'em. Part of the scene. Joy boys with expense accounts fly up from Frisco, down from Portland. Some from farther away. It's quite a layout. I'll show you if you want."

"No. I just wondered about Donetti. I met him, you know."

"Everybody knows, Johnny. After the wreck, when I picked you up in the car, I asked Marino about you. He seemed surprised. About the wreck. I told him your name. He said he'd offered you a job and you turned him down." She flopped over on her stomach, rested her head on a bent arm. Her eyes were inches from mine. "What are you doing here, Johnny? You come with my husband? From his friends in Frisco?"

"You too, huh?"

"Yes, me too." She blew a strand of hair out of her eyes. "Everybody likes to know where they stand. I don't even know who he worked for, whether he has any money coming—nothing. Where does that leave me?"

"I wouldn't know, doll. But believe it, you got no worries from Johnny Berlin. Except…"

"Don't," she said. "I'm serious. If you came to help him, say so. Then maybe I can make a move and know what I'm doing."

"Why don't you sit tight," I said. "Somebody'll be here from the outfit that bank-rolled the joint. They'll take care of you. Somehow."

"That's not good enough, Johnny." She sat up, put her spread hand on my chest. "Look, man. Don't hold out, huh? If you can steer me, I'll appreciate it. And I'll prove it."

"No kidding, Gina. I'm an innocent bystander."

The eyes got hard for a moment. Then she mustered a smile that didn't mean much. "Okay, Johnny. If that's the way you want to play it."

I sat up, swung my legs over the bed. I leaned on my thighs, looked out of the big window at the gently moving lake, rippled by widening wakes from motor boats and water skis.

"You better check at the hotel," I said. "See who's running the show. And find out about the operation upstairs—the broads."

"An assistant is running the place. He'll take care of everything. I wouldn't know what to do. And 'the broads,' as you call them, aren't upstairs. They have cottages. And you know them better than I. You had one on your lap in the Club Carroll."

"The redhead? Sheila? Well, what do you know…"

I stepped on it back to town, got there about six. Dan would be having a fit, trying to locate me. There are always a thousand and one last-minute details.

Condi answered the phone at the club. He told me Dan was running around like mad, wanted to see me as soon as possible. I told him I'd be there in about an hour, after I cleaned up.

The barber shop had an opening and I got it. The man was slick and expert so I went for a shave, massage and trim. It was six-thirty when I got to the Kenyon, took the ancient elevator to my floor. The corridor was deserted and the heavy, impersonal silence of a small-town, second-rate hotel hung there. I walked slowly down the long hall, scuffling my shoes on the worn runner. No reason why I should feel low. Good job, excitement in the offing. All kinds of good-looking broads around. What else is there?

But I did feel low. An awful lot of years had gone down hotel corridors, rolled across green baize tables, dissipated sugar-like in sweaty bedrooms, heavy with the unmistakable odor of sex. I tried to think of a joke to match the mood, something funny to remove the lingering melancholy that for damn sure wasn't usual with me. All I could think of was a man bleeding and a young girl crying.

I stuck my key in the lock. Another hotel, another empty room.

Only this one wasn't empty.

The first thing I saw was a smooth, well-tailored back; a small man wearing a hat. He was calmly tearing the hell out of my bureau. He didn't even look up when I kicked the door wide, stepped through cursing like a trooper.

"Don't get loud."

The voice came from behind me. Another one, who I hadn't been able to see behind the opening door, had a black gun clutched in one rock-steady hand. My belly fluttered and tightened where the snout pointed.

"Stand right there and don't get loud," the one with the gun said.

He was young, tall and hard-looking. He wore a month's salary in gray worsted and a light-weight hat, white shirt and a subdued tie. A hoodlum. But a real bad one. Young, but bad as hell. I could tell and you can bet your life I didn't get loud; I didn't get anything. The gunman leaned against the door, watched with cold eyes as his partner threw my shirts around.

I had no idea who they were or what they might be looking for. The searcher was another one. Cut from the same mold. Smaller, more deadly. He was about five-and-a-half-feet tall, dark and wasp-waisted; his nose was huge and he had a squint for little, jet-black eyes under heavy brows. I cleared my throat and he turned.

"Sit down," he said. His voice was a bass rumble.

I sat. The kid nudged with the cannon. He didn't need to. I sat and I burned. But I sat.

After a minute, I said, "You guys cops?"

I knew they weren't, but I figured I could put them on the defensive by mentioning law. No dice. They were pros. I didn't even get an answer. They had a job to do and they went about it calmly and expertly.

It didn't take long. The little one finished tearing up the place, kicked through my suits which lay on the floor. Then he walked over to me, stood looking down. His face told me nothing.

There was a knock on the door. I jumped. Literally. In a situation like that, any noise is a bad noise. For the first time in my life, I was hoping the cops had come for me. I twisted in the chair, watched Laughing Boy at the door. He didn't seem surprised. He reached behind him without taking his eyes off me and pulled the door open.

A short, flawlessly dressed man stood there, smiling under a gray, military mustache. He was poised and assured, with the trim, stocky figure you get from daily squash and workouts on the rubbing table. Flannel suit, white shirt, small-figured tie—even a cane. He stepped into the room, took off his roll-brimmed hat. He looked for all the world like a bank executive.

"You are Mr. Berlin," he said and it wasn't a question.

"I'm Mr. Berlin. And what the hell's the idea? I walk in, find these refugees from lineup ruining the joint. What gives?"

He smiled. A patronizing smile that really didn't say anything. He walked around the room; there was no doubt as to who was the boss. He had a fringe of white hair surrounding pink scalp and he rubbed it mechanically as he looked over my shattered domain.

"I'll be with you in a moment, Mr. Berlin. Have patience."

He looked at me directly. He had eyes like soft-boiled lemon drops. Except for them, he made a perfect picture of a successful banker or stock broker. He called the small man aside, his name was Marc, and the two conferred. Marc murmured and the older man nodded.

I could sit there all night and nobody would tell me anything. I got tired of it. What could they do anyway, kill me?

"Hey," I said. "I got a job. We open a new show at the joint where I work tonight and I'd like to be there. Is that reasonable? And if you'll tell me what the hell you're looking for, I'll give it to you."

The banker turned. "Yes, Mr. Berlin. That would be the Club Cherbourg, wouldn't it? Yes, Dan Gurion, I believe. Well, bear with me, please. I'll guarantee you will not miss your opening." He brushed a bent forefinger over the clipped hairs on his lip, nodded. "You'll get there, I'm sure."

He crossed quickly to the window, held the slats of the blind apart with the polished tip of his cane. A watch with a band of what looked like solid platinum glinted on his wrist. All he needed was a tall glass and a Dalmatian.

"Nothing but the gun, Marc?"

"That's all, Mr. Gilbertson." The small man's voice was flat. "Hasn't been fired. Nothing else of interest. Except maybe the kit."

"Kit?"

Marc shrugged. "He's a dealer. Got a hustler's kit. Dice, cards…"

"I see," the banker said. He rubbed his pink scalp for a moment, looking at the floor. Then, "Mr. Berlin, get dressed for work. We'll take you."

I did and they did and wow! The guy, Marc, must have been a race driver. He tooled the big car through the tricky curves of the Clover Canyon Road like it was the Salt Flats at Bonneville. If I hadn't been so busy answering the questions the banker put to me about Donetti's murder and the events leading up to it, I'd have been scared green.

It wasn't all one-sided. I found out, and it was about time, that Marino Donetti really had been playing with fire. He was Syndicate. So were my banker friend and his Ranger Platoon.

Donetti had advanced a plan for tying up the area. The whole thing. All gambling, prostitution, what have you. His Gambler's Protective Association was to have been the opening gambit.

Somebody checked him in one move.

And that's what my three escorts had come to find out. Who pushed Donetti. What they'd do when they found out wasn't hard to figure. A little guy in the syndicate gets dead. Comes immediately the flying corps because when you're with it, brother, you are forever with it, and nobody leans too hard without bringing down the wrath of the organization. I got the idea they didn't care so much about Donetti; it was the principle involved.

Some principle. Kick my cat, I'll kill your whole family.

CHAPTER TEN

T he Club Cherbourg was in for quite an evening. The parking lot was jammed. The streets adjoining the building were
solid with parked cars, as was the motel driveway and the apron
of the service station across the way. Even the weather was in
Dan Gurion's favor. The night was soft and warm and the stars
seemed glued to rooftops in a sky so dark blue you could almost
feel its nearness.

"By the door, boss?"

The banker came out of his reverie at the small man's over-
the-shoulder query.

"Yes, Marc. That will do. Mr. Berlin can get out here."

I said, "It's been nice. Just remember what I've told you.
I'd like to have somebody believe I wasn't imported muscle for
Marino Donetti."

"Yes. Well, there'd be no doubt of that in my mind, of course.
Mr. Donetti asked for no aid. He was confident he could deliver
the area himself."

"If you run into a cop named French, tell him that, will you?"

Marc laughed. The kid just sat there. My well-dressed friend
smiled in the darkness of the back seat as the heavy car swooped
to a stop in front of the Cherbourg. He spread his coat, slipped a
card case into his hand. He handed me a square of cardboard; my
thumb felt engraving on it.

"You were wise to be cooperative, Mr. Berlin," he said. "I don't
know if you had anything to do with Donetti's untimely death.
But I shall find out. What did you say that name was again?"

I pushed open the door. "Johnny Ronns. Or Blounce. Or something like that, and that's the best I can do. The guy had a hole in his neck."

"Quite." He cleared his throat, leaned across the back seat as I stepped to the roadway. "Don't do anything silly, Berlin. I'm inclined to believe you at the moment. But consider this—I intend to find out. There isn't the slightest doubt that I shall."

The knobby-muscled kid moved up beside me, stood there. A car swept up, blew its horn and whizzed past. I nodded at the banker.

"Okay. Thanks for the lift."

"Not at all. At the moment I am in your debt." His lemon-drop eyes gleamed in the early dark. "Keep it that way, Berlin. I rather like you."

A car horn blared behind us, lights stabbing forward. I stepped back and fingered my card. The kid jumped in and the big car gunned suddenly, roared away, heaving at the corner. I stood there for a moment. The night was cool enough, but a fine dew of sweat had misted my forehead. These people were bad. I knew it. It wasn't the first time my line of work had put me in contact with the octopus organization known variously as the Syndicate, the Combination, the Big Net, and other names less complimentary.

I looked at the card. The flashing club sign provided plenty of light to read the print: Horace Atkinson Gilbertson—Gilbertson Enterprises, Incorporated. There was a Portland address, phone number, but I'd seen plenty.

These were the big leagues. I never could hit a good curve. I wiped my forehead, walked to the door of the club. Gilbertson, huh? Somebody really was going to get hurt.

Dan met me just inside the door.

"Johnny. Where the hell have you been?" He came toward me, light glinting off his glasses, catching streaks on his face where sweat stood forth. "Christ, I'm swamped. I've had to do everything. Look at this crowd. Look at it."

"I'm looking." I grabbed his arm, pushed through the mob. The trio was working smoothly on the stand and the dance floor was full. "That's what you wanted, wasn't it?"

Dan stopped me near the Game Room entrance. He rubbed the silk lapels of his dinner jacket. "Well?"

"Real good job, Dan. All you needed was the idea."

He beamed. Then he told me about my part of the action.

He'd hired a kid from Welles to deal the twenty-one snap; put Fran and Bev on the crap table. Action was slow, would be till the people got used to our good music—and Laddy Layton.

The trio managed a fanfare that shook the chandelier, announcing the first show. Layton, immaculate and very vital out under that probing spot, spread his arms wide. The applause was tremendous. The mike dropped down and he began to sing. He was good, the bastard. Real good. He took over that crowd like a chorus cutie at a smoker.

Dan was grinning so hard his face looked strained. I punched him lightly, walked into the crowd.

Everyone seemed to be having a ball but me. But then maybe I cared about who killed Donetti more than anyone else. For at least two excellent reasons—my health and Gina.

Fran watched me furtively, peeking sideways when she figured I wasn't looking. She ran the table real well. Tonight she wore an icy-lime thing that clung to her firm body like skin, hugging the solid curves, dipping where it ought to. The blonde hair was feathered and combed forward, framing her features like a cap of creamy lather in a half-finished shampoo. Everything was fine except the tiny line between her eyes, the suggestion of a frown. I'd never seen her without it.

"How is it, Fran?" I moved behind the two girls, spoke over her shoulder.

She nodded, saying nothing. Her neck was bare quite a ways down and as I watched a dull red began where the dress ended and swept upward to meet her hairline. She rapped the stick hard on the layout.

"Ten," she said, her voice much harsher than I remembered it. "Mark ten, easy. Line and money ten. Field roll…"

I grinned at Bev who turned to nod at me. She winked, turned back to the game. I tapped her shoulder.

"Go powder your nose. I'll take it a while."

"All right, boss," she said, handing me the stack of chips in her hand. "Can I have a raise? I'm working like a good little dog."

"The comes go, Mr. Berlin," Fran said icily. "On and off."

She ran the game, ignored me. And the joint continued to jump.

Laddy Layton, like he'd said he would, was killing the people. During the second show the Game Room emptied except for a pair of die-hard blackjack players. We knocked off for a while.

"Quite a night, huh?" I said, when Fran and I had lit smokes, settled to rest.

She leaned against the table, slumped wearily. She hadn't yet spoken to me directly.

"Fran, what's wrong?"

She looked up. "Nothing. Too many people, I guess. Pretty good night."

"Pretty good? You ever seen a better since you've been in this hillbilly joint?" I picked up the hasp, slid the money-catcher in view. It was almost full. "Look at that."

"I see," she said. Then, suddenly flaring, "What do you want me to do—write a press release?"

I stopped, rose slowly, pushed the box back in with my knee. I looked at her for a silent minute.

"No," I said quietly. "I don't want you to do anything at all. Sorry I did whatever it was I did that got you down on me."

"Johnny, I—" She stopped, compressed her lips.

My hand touched hers; I fumbled for her fingers. Her eyes filled. Just like that. Then she jerked her hand away, fled through the door into the club proper.

I turned to Bev, who'd taken in the whole play. "What'd I do?"

She pushed her shoulders up, grinned a little wearily. "If you don't know, I can't tell you."

"Bev, look, I'm tired. I had a bad night. A guy gets shoved and I'm in the middle of it. Tough cops use me for practice. Everybody and his shill is trying to fit me to this local hassle." I flipped my cigarette end into the sand um. "I got no time for temperamental employees. So, tell. Tell quick and simple and don't worry about confidences. What the hell's with that girl?"

She shook her curls at me wonderingly. "Thought you were sharp, Johnny. And I guess maybe you are, in your own funny way. She loves you, that's all. She wants a chance to worry about you so you tell her funny jokes. She wants recognition as a woman, you give her funny dialogue." She shrugged. "Keep it light, keep it unimportant—keep it anything but real."

"You're out of your mind. She's an icicle, for Christ's sake."

"An icicle, huh? Boy, you know a lot about women."

"Look, I've only known her a couple days." I walked to the door, looked out at the main room. "How come it's got to be so big?"

"Because it's a big thing," Bev said softly. "Bigger than anybody, sooner or later. You'll see. Everybody knows about you and Gina Donetti." Her eyes turned away from me. "Fran, too. She digs you, you see. Maybe she wonders how you could make it with Gina fifteen minutes after her husband got dead."

"So that's it."

"Yes, that's it. You haven't changed, Johnny."

"Hell no, I haven't changed. Why should I?" A pair of loggers appeared in the doorway. "Take care of business," I told her.

I went to the bar.

Condi told me sometime during the evening that French had given him fits about the gun. The .45 used on Donetti had been one of Condi's. It seems he kept a large and lethal collection of the things in his motel cabin across the way from the Cherbourg. Everybody in the world, it seemed, knew about his passion for guns. French had traced it even though the bartender hadn't reported it missing. Each firearm had been registered as it was acquired and a ballistic sample taken, so French had no trouble running it down. But he'd let Condi go. He had been at the Club Carroll when the Cad hit the building. But so had everyone else in town. Or so it seemed. Condi just liked guns. Well, there's no accounting for taste.

Then I called French, asked if there was anything new and told him about Horace Gilbertson, my banker friend with the private army.

"Nice crowd."

I was next to the wall, the last stool on the bar's curve. Ford Messner had taken the one next to me, quietly moving in. I turned all the way around. His cold eyes swept on, over me, looked at the wall behind. His lips held a smile, but I knew how much that meant. He said, "I said, nice crowd."

"I heard you. What do you want here? It must be pretty important to make you wear a tie."

He looked down. He did in fact have on a tie, and the knowledge seemed to surprise him.

"You are a funny, Berlin. Ha, ha."

He pronounced the syllables carefully. I rolled up a fist, got a leg under me. His eyes narrowed.

"You want trouble, Messner? That what you came here for?"

"No trouble," he said finally. "Just looking around."

And he turned away. But his eyes said something else. For just a moment they spelled murder in chips of ice. It was there, then gone. Naked and shining, like minnows in blue water.

The evening was so hectic I didn't notice when he left. Like I couldn't remember when Carla Teacher came in, exactly. She came with a crowd of young people, none of them over twenty. The kids managed to get a table near the dance floor. I caught the waitress as she left the station, told her who I was and what I wanted.

"Just keep your eye on that kid, will you, honey?" The waitress balanced the tray of Cokes the kids had ordered, dodged traffic as we spoke. "I got a feeling about that girl and I want to know if anyone—aw, I don't know. Just watch her. Okay?"

"Sure, Mr. Berlin," the waitress said. "Where'll you be?"

"Game room, probably. Or the office. I'll be around."

The girl nodded, spun into the crowd expertly, balancing her loaded tray.

Then I forgot all about the incident because this was like get-away day at a country fair.

The Cherbourg was launched. If Dan maintained a policy of consistently good entertainment, reasonable food prices, he'd be home free.

The back room did fine. I gave the kids a break, then sloughed the twenty-one snap about one o'clock, put the hairy young man on the crap table with the girls. Dan and I started upstairs for a preliminary check of the receipts. We ran into Coley O'Rourke. He was with the redhead from Devil's Lake—a strangely chastened and penitent Sheila. She dropped her eyes when our paths crossed at the bottom of the enclosed stairwell.

"Hello, Sheila. O'Rourke."

Coley glared, pulling possessively on the girl's creamy arm. She stopped.

"I'm sorry about the other night, Johnny," she said.

"Keep quiet, Sheila," O'Rourke said. "This guy's a louse and you don't owe him nothing."

I got his tie in two fingers, twisted; his feet scraped and he came right up into my grin.

"Where's your memory, creep?" I asked. "You forget what happened to Parisi already?"

"Damn you!"

His skinny arms flailed. Dan moved in front of us, shielding the bit from the paying customers. I held O'Rourke's tie with my left hand, slid my right hip out of the way and jabbed four fingers of my right hand into his gut. He sagged; I held him up with the tie. The girl's face was white.

"Please don't, Johnny," she said. "Please don't. You'll make it hard on me."

The last was whispered in my ear as I turned O'Rourke to the wall, pinned him there face-first. The girl tugged at my arm. Her lipstick was as red as I remembered it and the pallor of her face made it stand out starkly. She was scared of something. Her lips trembled. "Please ..."

I let go of the club owner. He turned, gagging, face a livid blob in the dark of the stairwell.

"You bastard!" he whispered. He shot a glance full of malevolence at the girl. "I'll show all of you. Wait. Just wait."

I sighed, tired of the whole mess suddenly. "All right, O'Rourke, you're not hurt. Just get out of here. And don't take it out on this girl. If you do, I'll send you to visit Mops Parisi. You understand?"

He nodded. His eyes were full of the hatred of the man who has been humiliated, must accept it. He wheeled out the door. Sheila grabbed his arm and he jerked away savagely.

"What was that all about?" Dan asked.

I stared after the pair. "I don't know. I wish I did. I can't figure that O'Rourke at all. He should be against syndication as much as any of you."

"He is. That's one thing I can say for him. He's fought it from the first."

"But he's got Messner working for him. And you fired Messner because he wanted the GPA. How do you figure it?"

Dan said, "I don't know. But I sure don't want anything to spoil what we've got started here. How do you feel about staying, Johnny? I need you. You can see that."

My mind was still with the scene we'd just played. I took Dan's arm, started up the steps to his office.

"I'll stay, all right. But I've got a grifter's hunch. And it bothers hell out of me."

"What is it?"

"I had some visitors tonight. A pair of hoodlums and a big wheel from the syndicate that backed Donetti."

"Why didn't you tell me?"

"Listen." I pushed open the door, stepped into the office. "Donetti just started things off. Somebody's going to get hurt real bad around here. And for some silly, God-damn reason, I wish I knew who ..."

Dan bit his lip, pulled off the glasses. "Why, Johnny? It's none of our business, is it?"

I looked at him; my face felt tight, cold. "I don't know, Dan. I don't know."

CHAPTER ELEVEN

A waitress brought hot coffee and Dan figured up a preliminary total on the cash. I had robbed the four registers and a
quick tabulation showed an amazing figure with a good hour still
to run. He was still counting when the door burst inward, hit the
wall. Fran stood there, breasts heaving.

"Johnny. One of the waitresses said to get you right away."

I spun from the chair and joined her at the door. I knew what
it was. Fran's violet eyes were dark and concerned.

"What is it?" Dan asked. "Trouble?"

"None of ours." I grabbed the girl's arm. "I'll take care of it.
We should get down there, anyhow—still crowded."

We sped down the stairs. I sent Fran to the game room.

"Johnny, if you're in trouble, I want to help."

"It's all right, kitten. Just something I cooked up. Go take
care of my loot."

She ran her eyes over my face for a silent moment, then nodded. The full lips tilted. "Okay, champ," she said.

So maybe she'd quit being mad at me.

Layton was on for the last show. The crowd was intent. I made
the table where Carla and her coterie had been sitting. Everyone
was gone but Carla and the waitress, who was bending over her.

The kid sat huddled at the untidy table, shoulders hunched,
her young face white and puckered around the eyes. Layton was
wowing the people. But for once he wasn't moving Carla.

"What's up?"

The waitress turned, relief plain on her features. "Boy, am I glad you got here, Mr. Berlin. This kid's a mess. I don't know what's wrong with her. She's been sitting here and shaking for ten minutes."

"Well, something must have happened. You see anybody messing with her?"

The girl said no and I slid into the chair next to the huddled Carla.

"What's the matter, honey? Come on, look around at me here."

She pulled away. "Let me alone. I'm all right. Just let me alone!"

She was far from all right. "Tell me what happened. Someone scare you? Carla, why don't you level with me? You know I won't let anybody hurt you."

She shook her head hard, started sobbing aloud.

"Oh, for Christ's sake." I tried to turn her to me. "Come upstairs with me, Carla. Will you do that?"

The waitress came back, hovered anxiously.

Carla sobbed, "No. Just let me wait till Laddy's done. Then I'll go home. I'll go home …"

"People are beginning to notice, Mr. Berlin."

And they were. Even Layton on the stand looked our way with the annoyed frown of the heckled performer.

"Okay," I said. "Get a cab. I'll put her in it. She won't tell me a damn thing."

"I won't go," Carla said, looking at me for the first time "Not till I see Laddy."

"You mean that jerk let you sit here all night and hasn't even spoken to you?"

She nodded, miserable again.

"Why that—" I stopped, knowing how much good it would do to loud talk the creep to this kid. "Carla, look. Why don't you let me send you home? Then when Laddy gets off the stand, I promise to make him get in touch with you tonight. Deal?"

She looked up, biting her lip. The thin wrists in my hands shook with little recurring shocks. This girl was really torn up about something. It's funny what a man will do to some women. Suddenly I didn't care about the Cherbourg, the syndicate or what people might think. I stood, smoothed the shining head with my hand.

"Come on, sweetheart. We'll get you home and in bed. You want to see Layton, I'll see that you do. That's a promise."

Her eyes blinked and some of the tension left her. She nodded.

"If you will, honest?"

"Honest," I said solemnly.

I picked her up in my arms, threaded through the curious mob to the door. The cab was waiting. Carla didn't say a word, just huddled in my arms, shaking with a hiccup-like shudder.

The cabbie took my fin and my instructions and climbed behind the wheel. Carla settled back in the rear seat, handkerchief crammed in her mouth.

She was scared damn near to death. I could see that. I didn't know why or what of, but I knew she was terrified. And I had a hunch, one I should have followed up right away.

But she was game, determined to play the tragedy right on out. I tried again, but she wouldn't tell me a thing; just shook her head and looked at me with those clean, wet, shining eyes. I waved the cab away and watched it go.

Fran took me home in her car. We stopped for coffee, talked a little. I finally found out why she was a crap dealer. Her father was an invalid. He'd been crippled several years before in a mill accident, losing part of both legs and one arm entirely. Fran was the only child.

"I could have done a lot of things, Johnny," she said. "But I knew I was good looking. Enough people had told me. And the hospital bill was so big. I went to work for Ford Messner, learned to smile and push chips around."

"No insurance?"

She nodded. "There was some. You'd be surprised how they word those things. And how hard it is to collect. We got enough for the hospital. But there was the specialist from San Francisco, and therapy."

Fran sipped her coffee, made a face. She wore a light coat of some woolen material, boldly cut with a high collar. Her tan showed well against the beige, the lime dress.

"How long you think you can stick with it?"

She looked up. "Not forever. I'd like to get married someday."

I grinned. "No prospects?"

"Oh, prospects. No engagements yet, if that's what you mean. I'm not too hard to please, or anything. Just that I want to be sure. Real sure."

I hid behind my cup. "What's the matter with George French? Besides his being a cop."

"You don't mean that," she said quietly. "It's a pose and a pretty poor one. But I like George. He's steady and certainly manly enough."

"He's manly," I muttered.

"But I don't love him."

"That's the bit, huh? All of me. Yours till the end of time. You itch and I scratch." I leaned forward over the table, took her hand. "You really sold yourself that bill of goods, Fran?"

Her fingers lay in mine. She didn't say anything for a moment. Then, wetting her full lips, she said, "Maybe you think it's a bill of goods. And I guess that's all right. I don't. Lots of people don't." She pulled her hand away. "What it comes down to, Johnny, is that I'm a small-town girl. I want to get married to a man I love. A man I expect to spend the rest of my life with.

Not just a couple of sticky hours followed by emotional hang-overs. That's..."

She trailed off, looked out the speckled glass of the diner's window. I lit a cigarette, handed it to her.

"Emotional hangover, huh? You figure that's what I've been having all my life?"

She bit her lip. "I don't know anything about you, Johnny. I'm not prying."

"No, but you'd like to." I shoved back in the chair. "All you good girls are alike. You want to know. You got to know. Christ, is that all there is—one big confession after another? It seems to me a hell of a way to start out life with someone."

"I told you I didn't want to know anything." Her voice got louder. "What makes you think you're a candidate, Mr. Berlin? How come you imagine I even want to pry into your private life? We were talking about life, that's all. You want one thing, whatever it is, and I want another. All right, so I'm a good girl. And I like the way your lip curls when you say it."

"Now wait..."

"No." She stood up, gathered her belongings. "We've been building up to this ever since we met. All right, I'm attracted to you. You're big and you're handsome and I like a whole lot of things about you. Maybe I'd like to see how it would be to have you make love to me. But I'm not going to do it. Because I'm a good girl." Her mouth twisted with the words, and tears came to her eyes, deep purple now in the harsh light of the restaurant. "Whatever you call it, that's the way I am."

I sighed. "All right. I'm sorry."

I paid the bill, ushered Fran outside. The night was cool, mist laying low on the ground. Wet streaks marked the asphalt of the highway. The little coupe was mottled with moisture. I stopped her as she was about to climb into the car. She turned, looked up at me.

"Fran. What do I have to do to be eligible?"

Her pupils seemed to shrink. She moved forward slowly, then stopped, never moving her gaze from my face.

"When you're eligible," she said, so low I could barely make out the words, "you'll know it. Take me home ..."

Who knows anything about women? Not me. By the time I got to the hotel and into my room, my head was buzzing. Big pictures of Gina, pouting and sensual; Sheila, flaming and vital; Fran, cool and beautiful and strangely more disturbing than the others, flipped around in my head. And I'd had no sleep for quite a while. The bed looked good. Real good. I got out of my coat, started water in the tub.

Somebody tried to tear the door down. Sounded like it, at least. I started cussing ten feet from the door and had worked up a good head of steam by the time I got it unlocked and the knob turned.

Lieutenant French straight-armed the door and shoved me back into the room so hard I stumbled. His face was flushed. Behind him was the young cop with the barn-door shoulders.

"What the hell?" I said.

"Shut up," French said evenly. "Just stand there and don't say anything. Not nothing. Got that?"

I nodded. He was hot. Wilder than a bookie with cramps. And with a terrible restraint clamping his actions. I sat carefully on the bed, bare-chested and erect. The McKaneville police tore my room apart. And the valet had just put it back to rights from the earlier visit with my banker friend.

I sighed. "Second time today, George."

"Shut up," he said, and the frisk went on.

They got the clothes I'd been wearing, including the pants I still had on, tagged them, put the whole mess in a white bag and sealed it. I had no idea what the thing was about. And French wouldn't tell me. He made me don a pair of slacks, a short jacket and off we went to jail.

Only one time he'd opened up. That's when the bluecoat had uncovered my brand-new .38 in the bureau drawer. French grabbed it, shoved it under my nose.

"This yours?"

"My own," I said. "For cracking walnuts."

"Come on, slicker. Never mind the clever dialogue."

I stood up. "You tell me a lot, French. You give me a lot of consideration. Bust in here, throw my stuff around like it was going out of style. Well, that's fine. Maybe you got a license. But help you don't get. That clear? Until I know what's going on, I don't say a word. Not one God-damn word!"

French stuck his jaw in my face, glared for a moment. Then some of the hardness seemed to drain out of him. His big shoulders relaxed.

"You'll talk downtown," he said.

And that's where we went.

We went through a somber anteroom right into the office of Police Chief Rolly Cline. I saw Laddy Layton, Mickey System, Dan Gurion and Bev huddled with Paul Carter and Coley O'Rourke as we went through. A cop stood to one side of the door.

The chief's office was long and narrow, with one dirty window on the far end of the narrow side. There was a desk, a big chair, several straight-backs, filing cabinets and a long, long radiator running the length of the room. It hissed.

Rolly Cline didn't dress the room up any. It was the first time I'd seen the chief of police. I wasn't impressed. He was a fat old woman in pants with wrinkles and a food-spattered blue uniform on which the gold braid had tarnished years ago.

"This is our man, George," Cline said as we entered. "He has that doomed look I've come to recognize."

French nodded, motioned me to a chair. "Yeah, sure, Rolly. You get the testimony of the others? Every one of 'em?"

"All except the Cole girl. She hasn't shown up yet, George. All right here, George—on the little tape. Now we'll get Berlin's."

"Now you'll get Berlin's what?" I got up from the chair. I push all right, but only so far. This, I figured, was far enough. "You'll get my lawyer if you don't tell me what this is all about. You got a charge?"

French sat down, pulled his pistol away from his hip. He looked tired. His eyes asked me to be reasonable, but I didn't feel like it. I didn't feel like anything in the world so much as planting a foot in the middle of Rolly Cline's fat chest and shoving.

French said, "Donetti gets killed. We care, you know? But we don't bust too many guts about it. Somebody else, we care more and we work harder."

I believe I knew then. How, I couldn't say. But a definite chill started at my sockless ankles, crept upward till my face had hardened, my eyes had lost the scratchy heat, frozen open on the tilted figure of George French.

"Like who?" I said and waited.

"Like Carla," the lieutenant said softly. "Seventeen and lovely—and dead."

In the background I heard the asthmatic wheeze of McKaneville's police chief. And the unmistakable whir of a tape recorder.

CHAPTER TWELVE

"You believe that I killed that kid?"

French sat on the edge of the desk facing me. Cline, with his little tape recorder, was obscured by the beefy lieutenant. But I knew he hadn't missed any of the dialogue.

"Tell me again about when she came to the club."

I told him. I'd already told him once in the most exacting detail. When it came to the part about me putting her in a cab and sending her home, he stopped me.

"You told her you'd get Layton to call her? Go see her, or something?"

"Look, she was torn up." I sat straighter in the chair, tried to explain. "It was merely a matter of avoiding an incident."

"Did you do it?"

"Did I do what?"

French sighed. "Did you give the message to Layton?"

Well, there it was. "No," I said finally. "No, I didn't. But what difference does it make, Lieutenant? I only wanted the kid to get out of there all right. I knew she was scared. But she wouldn't say a word. Not a word. I did what I could."

"You know how she died?"

I shook my head, looked up at the boring eyes of George French. His slabbed face had lost some of its color.

"Run over three times with a heavy car," he said, voice flat. "Back and forth with a car. In her hand she had a note. From Laddy Layton. Anyway, signed with his name. The note said for her to meet him there, at Gypsy Hill."

"Gypsy Hill?"

"Local lover's lane. On the way in from Edson. Overlooking Clover Canyon."

I rubbed my eyes. "Such a pretty kid. No reason for it. None at all."

"Lots of reason, slicker. And you know what it was. You know better than anybody."

"You mean Donetti's push?"

"That's what I mean. You said she heard more than you did. Looks like you were right."

"What time?" I asked. I had to work to keep my mind operating. The shock was catching up with me. Maybe it was silly, but I felt responsible for Carla's death. I couldn't shake it. French said something. "What time?" I asked again.

"I told you," he said. "Medical examiner says about three-thirty, four. And one thing more."

"One more thing? What else could there be?"

"The note was scrawled on a napkin," the lieutenant said softly. "A Club Cherbourg napkin."

She had been found by a roving patrol making a routine check of the area. A car had run over the girl's soft body several times, tearing it almost beyond recognition. It was a very brutal way to kill.

"Answer my question," I said, rising from the chair. My face must have been tight because French leaned back, slid his hand around to his hip. "Answer me, French. You think for a God-damn minute I had anything to do with this kid's—with this God-damn—"

"Take it easy, Berlin." He took my arm, sat me down again. "I know how you feel. She was a nice little girl. Had no business within ten miles of this mess. But that's the way it goes. Now we have to find out who did it."

"That means you don't think I did."

"You were with Fran." The big cop frowned, turned away. "You wouldn't say so if it wasn't so. You know we'll check and she wouldn't lie. That leaves you out. But you're mixed in this thing somehow. I want your help."

"You got it. Anything at all and I'm not kidding. For once in my life," I added, very low.

French slid off the desk, got a notebook from his coat pocket. Rolly Cline started whispering to him. I caught a few words. The chief wanted it to be me. He said so. French shut him up, motioned me over to the desk.

"Here's the testimony we've got so far. Listen to it. Remember it. Then if there's anything you know you haven't told me, for Christ's sake, now's the time."

"Okay. Spin the thing."

The tape had the stories. Chunks of people's lives, different people, dissimilar people. All brought together because someone's greed had boiled over into violence. After the reel had run out, French lit cigarettes for him and me, settled in the swivel chair.

"There it is," he said. "I was busy running down a tip on the name thing. Remember Johnny Ronns? Nothing. I wasn't here when the call came in."

Through the spinning smoke we got it all laid out. The working theory was that Carla had heard Donetti name his killer just as he was going out. She'd known her information was dynamite. Maybe even received a warning. That would account for her strange behavior in the Cherbourg last night. Anyhow, she was scared enough to know that what she had heard could kill her. Nothing in the world could have got her to that spot on Gypsy Hill but a note from Laddy Layton. Once there, the killer had eliminated the possibility of Carla exposing him. Permanently.

Both Dan Gurion and O'Rourke were clean on preliminary investigations. Dan by his wife's testimony and O'Rourke because he'd been with a party including Paul Carter, the owner of the Club Carroll, and several others. French said it was tight. Bev had been brought in only because she had been with Condi Capucho, the Cherbourg's pistol-loving bartender. He was a natural suspect because his gun had killed Donetti. And for another reason I hadn't known about. He was a pimp. Yeah, a pimp. That's why he could afford an expensive collection of guns. You never know. It surprised me, that's all.

Bev King alibied the bartender. They'd been having coffee till four in a joint downtown. They could prove it. Mickey System had been in the same place and could also prove it. He'd left the Cherbourg and met Bev and Condi at the coffee joint.

Mickey was also a pimp. That didn't shake me nearly as much as finding out about Condi. The little system player had always seemed a hair too rubbish to be true. I wasn't surprised to find out he had a girl in Welles, the lumber port thirty-five miles north where Dan and I had stopped for coffee on the way back from Portland.

There was nothing on the tape about Ford Messner. Nothing on Gina Donetti. And not a word about Horace Gilbertson and his two cold hoods.

"That's all, huh?"

French looked up from examining the thinning sole of one shoe. "That's all. Except I called Mrs. Donetti—" he glanced at me, then away—"to check on her and the guy from Portland, that Gilbertson. She didn't know about him although I've got information that he's headquartered at the lake. But she had a solid alibi. Or so it seemed."

"She need one?"

"Everybody needs one." French studied his closed fist for a moment, then he rose abruptly and walked to the window. He stood there with both hands in his hip pockets. "And I'm a sonofabitch if everyone hasn't got one."

The phone rattled on the desk. French turned, scooped, cuddled the instrument against his face.

"French. Yeah, send her in when I buzz."

He dropped the phone onto the cradle, looked at me. His eyes were bleak and unfriendly again.

"Fran," he said.

"The tape told me one thing, Lieutenant. You want to hear it?"

He chewed his lip a moment, then shook himself all over. He got out his book, settled on the edge of the desk again.

"Yeah, slicker. I want to hear it. Shoot."

"I know what Donetti said when he died."

Cline choked, dropped a reel of tape. French leaned forward. "You mean you know who the murderer is?"

"No. I didn't say that. Only that I know what he said now. It was the tape. Hearing about the pimps around here. I never thought about it—never knew there was so much organized prostitution, for that matter. But that's what he said when he died."

"What are you talking about, Berlin? You said you heard the guy mention a name. Johnny Ronns or Blounce, you said. Or something like that."

"Johnny Ronce," I said.

French looked at me blankly. Cline cursed petulantly and flicked off the recorder.

"That means something, I guess. But I'm dumb, slicker. Lay it out for me."

"Rhyming slang. Limey rhyming slang, only it isn't only Limey now. We picked it up from them. But the English used it first and best. Pimp is ponce. They rhyme it Johnny Ronce—for ponce—which is pimp."

French scratched his head with the eraser end of the yellow pencil. "Ponce," he said, the idea growing in his eyes. "Could be. And ponce. All right, Johnny Ronce. Instead of the word pimp or fish, or fish and shrimp like we do it in this country."

"That's the bit," I said. "Johnny Ronce. An Englishman would say it like that."

"Did you know Donetti was a naturalized Englishman?" French asked.

"No. But I remembered there'd been something about the way he talked, some little flavor that I couldn't identify that night on the highway. The first night I got here. Anyway, I heard Donetti say something like that. Johnny Ronce. And when I heard the pimp, pimp, pimp tonight, it clicked." My cigarette had burned down to my fingers. I looked around for an ashtray, finally dropped it on the floor. "The use of the slang is widespread. Especially in the circles I travel. Hustlers and dealers, bartenders and fringe people. But it's a little different from the English variety even though that's where it came from originally."

French said, "I know, I've run into it. Pimp would be fish— for fish 'n shrimp." He grinned, the movement transforming that beefy face. "And bottle—for bottle and stopper. Meaning copper. Yeah, I've heard it, all right. But I never would have made the connection like you did with what you heard."

"It had to be. There was no one else in the thing named anything like what he said. I'm the only Johnny. And I know damn well I didn't do it. When you couldn't uncover something, I wondered if my ears had been tricking me. But that's what he said. Johnny Ronce. He was cussing his attacker. He probably called to Carla, who was outside for some air. Remember, he was dying and he knew it. I think he wanted to use that gun he had on whoever it was that had used it on him. He told the girl to get someone from the club, called him a God-damn Johnny Ronce just because he was dying and knew it and crazy mad to get some skin before he cashed in. That's the only way it figures."

"Maybe you think so. But I need evidence. What reason does that leave for Donetti's push?"

"Lieutenant, I don't know that. Maybe the protective association thing he was trying to push. Maybe the syndicate didn't like the way he was running things at the lake. Maybe he was getting ambitious. Hell, I don't know. Maybe any God-damn thing. You figure it out."

French considered it. "No," he said. "That isn't it. It's local. I'm sure of that and I'm sure the same guy killed both Donetti and the girl. And I'll find out who."

He rose, motioned the chief to turn off the machine.

"You go on home, slicker. We'll see about—"

"Wait a minute. How about Ford Messner? And what's with the girl Sheila? How come you haven't mentioned them?"

"Sheila works at the Devil's Play Spot. We know that. But it's outside our jurisdiction."

"Never mind alibiing the vice. What about Messner?"

He looked at me for a moment like he'd like to tear my head off. For the first time I got an inkling that it might not be easy to be a cop. Especially an honest cop in a dirty town.

"Okay," he said. "Sheila's Messner's girl. She—"

"That's what I wanted to hear. That makes that chilly bastard eligible and I like the hell out of that."

"Wait. That's why he's working for O'Rourke. Coley has eyes for the redhead. Always had. He figures by having her old man around he puts himself in a position where he might get aced in. You see?"

I nodded. "Yeah. I worried about that. Him working for O'Rourke. Coley was supposed to be against this GPA thing and Messner was pushing it. And Messner was on the scene real quick when Donetti got it. Real quick."

"He followed you out."

"He says."

"Who says different? Nobody knows who was in and who was out when the Cad hit the building. And what difference does it make, anyhow?"

"I like him," I said stubbornly.

"You mean you don't like him. That's fine. I don't like you." His eyes swung around, settled on my face. "But I won't fit you for a murder rap for that reason."

"But he's—"

"He's got an alibi, Berlin. A good one."

"Not for the Donetti push."

"No. But for Carla. He was with a girl. Till after four. Pretty hard to shake."

"Sheila? You'd take her word? Why that's the—"

His head was shaking. He leaned back, gripped a knee in both hands. A funny little smile played around his hard lips.

"Not Sheila," he said. "She was with Kilgallen all the time. Messner was with Gina Donetti. Till four in the morning."

Fran got me out of there. The days without sleep caught up with me all at once. The shock of finding out about Carla didn't help any. And the bit about Messner and Gina. All together it was too much. My mind just got soggy and dark; the world slid back a little and I watched things happen without taking part myself. I don't know what French said to Fran. I don't know what she told him about us. I was there, but my abused mind and body had decided it was time to recuperate.

The world was still the same. The same stinking boxes within larger stinking boxes calibrated according to chance, each with a corner reserved for private hells. This was the first I'd ever inhabited. Why Carla's death should affect me this deeply I couldn't imagine. I only knew that it had. Perhaps I'd been getting ripe for this a long time. Maybe my dissatisfaction with Reno and Vegas and the merry-go-round I'd been riding for years had finally become too much for me. It's a hell of a life.

But she was dead. Torn, bloody dead. When you die, it's a long time between drinks.

And Gina was Messner's alibi.

Someone was slapping my face. The morning came to me with a rush. It was Fran. Her ivory loveliness swam into focus and I looked around.

"What goes?"

"Your hotel, Johnny. You tried to walk past. I didn't want to take you inside."

I backed off, looked at her. No frost this morning. Cream slacks and a suede coat over a tight sweater. Her short hair was mussed and ragged around her face.

"That figures, you wouldn't take me up."

"Johnny, don't start that again. It isn't what I meant."

"It's what you said."

"I know, but—" She sucked a breath, stuck out her chin. "Look, I only meant I didn't want anyone to—to—"

I said, "To what? Go ahead, to what? You think so damn straight you couldn't bend to save a life. Or a soul."

Tears formed in her eyes, dimming the violet lights. "Johnny, I don't know how to act with you. I just don't. I'm not trying to act the perennial virgin, really I'm not."

I closed my eyes. "Go home," I whispered. "Get away from me. You don't belong here. You don't belong with me. Any more than that kid belonged with Layton."

"Oh, Johnny, have you been blind all your life? Don't you think if you cut me I'll bleed? If you play on me, music will come? I can't help what I am. I love you, God help me, but I can't be anything but what I am."

Her breasts rose sharply with her breathing, pushing aside the wings of her coat. Her face was white, strained.

"I can't be Gina Donetti, Johnny. Even for you."

I slapped her. My hand came up and I slammed her against the glass. The moment it was done, I was sorry. But I couldn't say so. The words wouldn't come. My brain ran sweat and a pain began behind my ears. Her head came around. There was no fear in her face, no recrimination. Just the sorrow and red marks from my fingers, my hand. Her eyes looked at me, openly, steadily.

I turned away.

Had to get to my room. To bed. Too long without sleep, too much emotional spending. I slogged to the elevator, wrestled open the doors. My eyes searched the lobby windows before the sliding panels cut off my view.

Fran was gone ....

CHAPTER THIRTEEN

The phone rang for a long time before I could force myself to answer it. A wad of crumpled and sour sheets made a lump under me. I rolled over, snatched the clanging instrument.

It was Gina. I came awake, swung my legs over the side of the bed. She was talking. I couldn't understand anything she said, so I told her to call back and hung up.

The ringing began again right away. I let it ring. I just dropped my head into my hands and sat naked on the soiled bed and thought of Carla. Carla—bright, like a new dime or old dreams. From now on she'd be a name, a twinge. That's all. So I sat there sweating in the airless heat of the afternoon in a cheap room of an earthy town and said my poor good-by. To a kid I'd hardly known. But she'd become important to me in a way I didn't really understand. Maybe wouldn't ever understand.

Twice while I shaved and cleaned up for the night's work I called the Devil's Play Spot, asked for Gina. She wasn't there. I called Dan and told him I'd be late that night.

Then I called French, asked if there was anything new on the killing and got the dead girl's address. The only thing French had found out since last night was that the murder car had been a stolen heap from Roseburg, an inland town about ninety miles away. They'd found it in a canyon, without recognizable prints.

My rented heap was still in the hotel parking lot. I filled it at a gleaming station, ate peanuts and drank a Coke. My stomach was empty; had been, it seemed, for days. But somehow I didn't want anything to eat. Not just then. Halfway to Devil's Lake the mist darkened and I switched on the headlights. The dash clock said six-twenty.

There were five or six cars in the graveled lot to one side of the main building. I squeezed in next to a low-slung sports car, stepped out into pine-scented night. A bright red grew all around me and I realized they'd turned on the sign atop the place. Business as usual. The king is dead; long live the queen. The flickering neon flames shed a diffused glow on the light mist, bathed the glittering hotel-casino in pink phosphorescence.

The lobby was almost empty. A clerk behind a fancy desk; a bored bellhop and a cigar stand with a leaning girl. I walked to the desk. It was small and compact sandwiched between two sweeping modern stairways. A redwood slab counter and rows of pigeonholes for mail behind it. The clerk told me where the office was and I took off across the lobby.

I walked what seemed like several blocks toward the lake side of the building. The hall was dark. Offices and dressing rooms. A red bulb glowed over a fire exit a few yards beyond the door I stopped before. I knuckled briefly.

"Come in."

I stepped in, closed the door. It was an office. Donetti's probably. Gilbertson was there with Gina. Both looked up at my entrance; neither spoke.

The room was coldly modern and efficient. A large ivory-colored desk and a profusion of leather chairs and a couple of green file cabinets. A small bar stuck out of one wall.

I said. "Howdy."

Gina came alive then. She flowed toward me, put up her arms, kissed me on the mouth. Like a long lost dividend or the hero come with the rent.

"Darling." The eyes went up and down, lids drooping. "Where have you been? I've been frantic."

"Where have I been?" I looked at her. The smooth face seemed unnaturally tight, rigidly controlled.

She took my hand, kept her eyes turned away from Horace Gilbertson, led me to a cream-leather couch. Her perfume, the heady aroma of crushed violets, drifted behind like a beckoning finger.

"Sit here, darling," she said. "I'll get you a drink."

The banker watched the bit, a tiny smile tugging at his mustache. He said the ordinary things and I replied. But I was watching Gina. Something about her nudged me differently than ever before. I didn't know what. But I'd find out. She hipped her way to the tiny bar. She had on a clinging jersey thing with a gold kid belt; her slippers were gold, too, and high-heeled. The raven hair hung loose as if she hadn't had time to arrange it. And maybe that was it. Maybe Messner had stayed longer than four o'clock this morning. Gilbertson was still talking. About the girl's death, about Donetti's leaving the affairs of the Play Spot in a mess.

Gilbertson seemed at home behind Donetti's desk. Or maybe he just seemed at home behind any desk. A silver modern drape hung behind the chair, outlining his head. A cold glass touched my hand and Gina folded herself neatly onto the couch beside me, crossed her legs with a nylon hiss.

"The Play Spot needs a manager," he said. "You have the experience. My reports on what you've accomplished at the Cherbourg in a short time are good."

Gina's hand caught my unoccupied one, squeezed it. I took a long drink of the Scotch and water, set the glass on the floor.

"Well?" Gina said. "Say something. Answer him."

"When I answer him, baby, I'll have something to say."

"What's to think about, darling?" She was hitting that kind of heavy, I thought, under the circumstances. "He just offered you the Play Spot. You know what that means?"

"I can puzzle it out." I pulled my hand free, leaned forward in Gilbertson's direction. "Mr. Gilbertson, thanks a lot, but no thanks. I got troubles without getting mixed up with you people."

"What do you mean, 'you people'?"

I shrugged. "We all know what I mean. I'm a loner. No ties. I'm stubborn. Somebody continually telling me what to do and how to do it, why I'm a cinch to mess up. You wouldn't be satisfied with me at all. And I don't like the operation here."

Gina snorted. "I do believe he means the girls, Horace. Damned if it hasn't got a conscience."

"I can see where you'd think that was funny, doll." I turned to her and I guess my eyes were cold; she backed away a little. "No conscience. I can't afford it. Just some things you do, some you don't do. That's all."

Gilbertson nodded. "Principles," he said. "Of whatever sort. I respect them. We'll let that go. What have you found out about the death of our—of Marino Donetti? And do you believe the young girl's death is linked?"

"Yes. They're linked, all right. No other reason for that kid to get it. That's why I came out tonight. It's about time somebody found out for sure why Donetti got shoved. I think you know."

He swiveled the chair slowly, made a tent of his fingers. His eyes were slitted and I thought they were aimed at Gina. She sat, saying nothing, plucking at the jersey dress where it dipped between her thighs. Restless. Eyes dark and the generous body molten and vibrant even in repose.

"Berlin," Gilbertson said suddenly, "I'm going to tell you."

I got up, walked to the bar, speaking over my shoulder. "One thing first. If it touches this kid's death, this Carla, I'm going to tell the cops if I think I should."

"All right. Your judgment. Do you have any ideas? Just to see how your mind works, Berlin. No games."

I poured a drink, walked around the couch and stood behind Gina, looking over her at my banker friend.

"No syndicate pressure. I know that. If you were trying to sew the area you'd do it right and you'd do it tight and there'd be no slips. Right?"

"Granting the premise," he said, smothering a smile. "Substantially correct. Go on."

"Leaves a couple of things. Donetti operating on his own, with or without permission from the—from you. A big debt of some sort is another possibility. And finally—" I looked down at Gina. She was still. The black dress began low and when she pushed her head back on the couch, looked up at me, I could almost see her navel. "Finally, this one," I said. "Gina. The bomb with a short fuse. Nature's answer to birth control."

Gilbertson nodded. Gina's eyes narrowed.

"I don't deserve that from you, Johnny," she said. "I can be nasty, too, you know."

"No offense, doll. But it's a possibility. Jealousy in any number of directions. Anyway, enough games. What's the bit?"

"Money," Gilbertson said. "Seventy-five thousand dollars."

I whistled. "Figures. The long green."

Gina sucked a sharp breath. "Horace, it doesn't figure. There's more than that here all the time."

"No, there isn't," Gilbertson said. "Close, sometimes. After a good weekend. We do not customarily allow that much money to accumulate in one spot. For obvious reasons. Besides, this was different money, for a different purpose. Small bills, unmarked. It was delivered to Marino Donetti by a representative of an organization in which I have a small interest. For a specific purpose."

"I got it," I said. "And a whole lot of other things. Now I know why I got run off the road the first night I got here."

"What do you think, Mr. Berlin?"

"Operating capital. To tie up the area for the syndicate."

"I don't like that word."

"Okay, company, then. Anything you want to call it. The whole works in a bundle. The gambling through the Gambler's Protective Association. The vice through muscle and key control with this joint as a nucleus. That it?"

"Substantially. Donetti submitted a plan. We looked it over, decided to let him go ahead on his own initiative. If he could wrap up this tight little area—and outside people would have run into much difficulty, Mr. Berlin, believe me—then he would be the logical man to run it for us." He shrugged. "It seemed worth a chance. We'd been thinking about it. We knew that small towns were tough. They band together against what they call foreign interests. If anything was to be done, it had to be done from inside. Donetti proposed to do that. He promised help from local sources."

I reached the desk in a stride. "That's what I want to hear. Who? Name me the local source and you can forget the hassle."

His eyes came up, met mine. They looked more yellowish in the full glare of the overhead lighting.

"We don't know," he said. "That's why I—we—are here. I propose to find out."

"You'll have to beat me."

"No contest, Berlin. I'm interested in the money. And in finding out who killed Donetti. If you help, I will, of course, be grateful. On the other hand..."

He let it trail off and hang in the room, but we all knew what he'd been about to say. I nodded, pushed my glass back and forth on the desk top.

"One more thing," I said, turning to the woman. "Before I go to work. What were you and Ford Messner doing here at four in the morning?"

Gina pulled her head off the couch-back, looked at me.

"You make it sound like an accusation, darling."

I spun, walked to her.

"No double-talk. No stalling. You think I'm jealous, you're wrong. You think I'm panting after your spot, you're wrong. I want to know because last night a little girl got killed for no reason that makes a damn bit of ordinary sense. So I want to know."

She lowered her eyes, twisted on the leather couch. "Certainly," she said. "Mr. Messner came here to ask me to intercede with Horace for him about the managership of the Play Spot. That's all."

"How long was he here?"

"Oh, what difference does that make? All you—"

"What time, Gina?"

"Four," she said, suddenly blazing. "There, you happy? He came about two and left after four. That's what I told the police. That's what I tell you. Now think what you please."

My eyes stayed on the perfect face, watching for some sign that would tell me which way to jump. There was nothing. Just the spurious anger, and maybe a little fear.

"Okay," I said. "That makes it damn convenient for Ford Messner. You give him a hard alibi. Without it, he'd be the number-one suspect for both killings. Damn convenient."

Gina rose swiftly, gripped the lapels of my coat. "Listen, Berlin. Whatever you might think of me, you can't believe I'd shield my husband's murderer."

I pulled away, walked to the door. Gilbertson got up from the desk, joined me there.

"I've got to go," I said. My chest burned.

"I'll walk with you," Gilbertson announced.

"Johnny," Gina said. "I want to talk with you. Can't you be a little late tonight?"

"I'm going to be a little late. There's a little gathering I have to stop in on." I got the door open, stepped out into the hall. Gina's face appeared in the opening after Gilbertson had followed me out.

"What are you talking about?"

I lifted her chin, looked down into the dark eyes. "About a little house in Wood Town with a wreath on the door."

Gina's face drained. She jerked away from my hand, slammed the door. The sound echoed in the long corridor.

"Mr. Berlin," Gilbertson said, as we walked. "The thing I want you to remember is that I'm quite serious about hiring you. If you change your mind, let me know."

"No chance," I said, adding, "Gilbertson, you could do worse than this Messner. He's a good dealer."

"I know. But I distrust the man. I distrust any man that lives off a woman."

"You know about that, huh?"

"Very little around I don't know about, Berlin. And I'll know more. But Messner is not my man. We'll bring in someone, like we did Donetti. I might tell you that Gina thinks as you do. She's been trying all day to get me to hire Messner. Would you say that was odd?"

It didn't shake me nearly as bad as good old Horace thought it would. I'd been expecting it, as a matter of fact.

"I'd say it was Gina coppering her bets. As usual."

Gilbertson nodded, stepped outside into the Oregon night as I held the heavy glass door.

"Probably," he said. "Remember this. Seventy-five thousand is not all the money in the world. But it hasn't been found."

"It's enough," I said.

"Enough?"

We stopped on the immaculate steps, watched the drifting tendrils of red-bathed mist.

"Yeah. Enough motive for murder. It looks to me like Donetti tied up with a local boy to ramrod this scheme. Then he requested operating capital. When it arrived, the partner decided a bird in hand was worth a hell of a lot more than a hustler's promise. So he got a gun, went rooty-toot in the bushes and was home free."

"That sounds workable," Gilbertson admitted. "Plus the timing. You met Donetti as he was meeting our messenger with the money. Someone saw you together. The natural assumption would be that you were our man, sent to protect our investment."

He grinned wryly in the artificial light. "Which wouldn't have been a bad idea, it now appears."

A lot of things got clearer then. The meeting on the foggy road, Donetti's proddy actions with me. His subsequent phone call to the Club Carroll which I hadn't answered.

I sucked a lungful of the cooling air.

"I'm hungry. I'll see you around. Tell Gina for me that she can quit trying. I'm not going to take the job."

Gilbertson brushed a finger over his mustache. His lemon-drop eyes glowed.

"I shall tell her," he said. "And I'll tell you something since you seem bent on messing in this thing. Find the girl Sheila. Talk with her. Perhaps she will tell you what we couldn't get out of her."

"Sheila?" I said, surprised. "What's she got to do with it?"

"Only this. Kilgallen works here, you know. He likes the girl. Well enough, in fact, to give her an alibi for the time of Carla's death." He clipped a cigar quickly, rolled it between pale lips. "Earlier today he confided in me. He was not, in fact, with the girl during the crucial time."

"Well, Sheila's here, isn't she? She works here."

"She left today. With her clothes."

"Did she see Messner when he was here?"

He shrugged. "I don't know. I don't know that Messner was here. Except that Gina says he was. At the moment I have no reason to doubt her. But to get back to the flaming Sheila. She is, I believe, deeply in the middle of this thing. I admit that I do not know how."

"I'll find out," I said. I walked down the steps to the graveled walk. "When I do, I'll let you know. Maybe."

"Berlin." I stopped, turned back. Gilbertson's compact figure was a dark blob against the lobby lights. "No maybe. Please believe this, I want to know."

"Okay," I said. "You'll know. But don't push on me, Gilbertson. Let me blunder in my own way."

I got the motor started, backed the Ford out into the driveway. Gilbertson waved from the porch, beckoned. I threw the heap in reverse, backed to the steps.

"What is it?"

He leaned down, peered in the open window. "What is that girl's address, Berlin? The one that got killed."

I looked at him. His pink features were difficult to read, but I thought I knew what he was feeling now. Crook or no crook. He spun the cigar in his lips absently, waited for my answer.

"Thirty-eight Belden Circle," I said. "They're burying her tomorrow."

"Good," he said. "If you need help, Berlin, call me here."

"I will."

A lush figure materialized behind the banker. Gina, still wearing that jersey dress that would have been against the law in Paris.

"Johnny," she said, "I told you I wanted to talk to you."

I leaned out the window, looked up at her. "I got things to do, kid. See you around."

She came down the steps, brushing past Gilbertson. Her perfume swept into the car, mixed with the rush of warming air from the rattling heater.

"Johnny, you don't understand." Her fingers gripped my arm. Her head came down level with mine. "I want you to come to the bungalow. I've missed you, darling. I want to see you. Badly."

I couldn't see her eyes, but by. now I didn't have to; I knew what they would be saying. I put the car in gear, touched my toe to the accelerator.

"Take a cold swim," I said, and roared out of there.

CHAPTER FOURTEEN

It was seven-twenty. I'd already made a flying visit to the Cherbourg. Now I drove the rented car along the beach road toward the Kilgore Hills. This was a suburban development, if McKaneville could be said to boast such, south and coastward of the town. Dan had told me Sheila had a small house there. On Crescenta Drive.

I found Crescenta Drive, all right. Kilgore was the main drag, running all the way from downtown, up the mountain and circling the development. Crescenta branched off this one, twisting oddly. The house wasn't hard to find, even in the fog.

It was a box affair, with canned lawn and do-it-yourself shrubbery, set back twenty feet from the street. There was no sidewalk. I got out, walked all around the joint. Nobody home. A window opened into what appeared to be a living room. I pulled it wider, peeked in. No sound. It was really empty. I noticed a film of dust on all the wooden surfaces. Sheila hadn't been home lately. The lawn was two inches too long. A collection of newspapers littered the porch. I tried the door, not knowing what else to do. It was locked.

Then I made the pilgrimage. And if you think it was easy, you're out of your skull. Wood Town—small houses and working people. I found the place.

I met a dewy sister, eyes still swimming with the dark syrup of grief; an older brother, balding and bewildered by the sudden loss; a mother and father, dry-eyed and stunned. It was a small house and my coming caused a ripple. The casket was closed. It was to stay that way. Mrs. Teacher met me at the door. Her eyes were dull and lifeless.

The people all looked at me. I stuck out in this joint and I should have been very uncomfortable, smarting with the knowledge that this was a part of existence I'd never known. But it didn't bother me at all. Not at all. I looked at the ugly box, the pitiful stacks of flowers; smelled the sickening, belly-gripping scent of funeral wreaths mixed with burning wax. Two enormous candles flanked the fancy box. It had brass findings. The furniture had been removed; folding chairs spaced about held the mourners. The candles were the only light.

"Did you know my—" the voice broke, went on. "Carla?"

He was a small man. Normally the checks would have been rosy, pushed out and full of color. Now they were sallow, pointing up thinning, graying, once-yellow hair.

"You're Mr. Teacher," I said. "Yes, sir. I knew her. Not for long and not very well. But I knew her."

Nobody said anything for a while. I could hear the chirping of a nightbird from outside; the faraway whine of a saw at the rough mill. I stood and closed my eyes and tried to remember the eager young face. I could not.

That night at the club. I'd put her in the cab. I could have brought her here, to her home. Where loved ones and the deep buried respectability of the neighborhood would have protected her. Instead...

I turned sharply from the closed casket, walked to the outer door. My throat was tight and the candle smoke was irritating my eyes.

"You're leaving, Mr ... uh ..."

"Berlin," I supplied, stopping at the door. Mr. Teacher and his wife followed. Their son and the remaining daughter crowded the parlor door. I could see curiosity pushing aside some of the grief and despair. "I work at the Club Cherbourg. I met Carla there briefly. She was a very nice girl."

The woman scrubbed her face against the man's chest and sobbed.

"Look," I said brusquely. "I didn't have time to get a wreath. I meant to. Please take this—" I got a bill from my wallet. "Do what you like with it."

"A hundred dollars?" Teacher looked up at me. "I can't take this, sir. Thank you just the same."

"You take it," I said. It was increasingly hard to talk. I wanted to get out of there. "Take it. And later someone will come with some more. A short man in a big car. You take that, too. You take it, hear?"

The door opened under my hand and I stepped onto the small porch. They crowded the doorway.

For the first time in my life I ran out of words. Clear out. My throat moved, but nothing happened. I bobbed my head at them, then stumbled off the porch and ran for the Ford.

The Cherbourg was loaded to the eaves. Twisting, sweating, laughing it up, a multitude of people with nothing better to do than manufacture their own Mardi Gras. Dan was doing fine. At this rate he and Bev would have that cruise; or whatever it was they wanted, pretty quick.

"Hi," a voice said.

I turned. It was Mickey System. His tie was again boisterous. His eyes were bright, the skin around them drawn tight. He wasn't grinning. Not a bit.

"Mickey. What's with it?"

"Bad about the kid, huh?"

"Yes. That's the way it always is. Somebody who hasn't got a thing to do with it gets hurt."

Mickey looked around, gripped my sleeve. "Look, Johnny. I know you won't believe this, but I gotta tell you. I'm with you.

You're trying to find out who pushed her. I'll help. Any way I can. I mean that."

I looked at him. His face was hard and the glaze had left the bulging eyes.

"How'd you know?" I asked. "About me looking for the killer?"

"It's around. You're looking for Sheila. You talked to that syndicate guy everyone's wondering about. Nobody else has, including the heat."

"You seen French?"

"I heard. He's in Roseburg. Checking out the car that killed the girl. Coley shut his joint down. Messner's out of work."

"Shut it down? Why?"

Mickey shrugged. "Who knows? Sheila, I guess. You know about that?"

"O'Rourke and Sheila? And her being Messner's old lady? Yeah. I know. Where is Messner?"

"I dunno." He moved close, murmured in low tones. "But I know you're messing in the thing."

"You know a lot for a guy who don't know nothing. Get away from me, hustler. When I want your help I'll let you know."

His eyes closed a little. Then he sighed. "Okay," he said. "I guess I got that coming. The offer still goes."

He spun and vanished into the crowd.

Condi nodded from behind the plank, beckoning with his chin. His double-black mustache wasn't twitching tonight. Everyone felt the loss of the girl, I guess. Whether they'd known her or not. You don't have to own the property to recognize waste when a house burns down.

"What, Condi?"

"Call for you. Several, Johnny. Some broad."

A tremor ran through my legs. "Who was it?"

"Nobody I recognized. Didn't leave a number. Where'll you be if she calls again?"

"Game room," I said. "Send me a double Scotch and water in a tall glass."

He nodded and I went into the back.

Players were three-deep behind the crap spread and the twenty-one snap was loaded. Guilt tugged at me. Dan Gurion, face flaming under his tan, worked the payout with Bev while Fran ran the game. The kid at the blackjack table was sweating and his eyes were strained. They'd all been working without letup.

I waved at Dan, motioned to the dealer to take a break and went behind the half-circle of baize and chrome.

The action was stiff and I hadn't dealt the card game in quite a while. One thing about twenty-one, it keeps a dealer awake. I flipped the plastic cards, rattled the chips and silver and thought about Sheila. What could the redhead know that everyone was looking for her? And who was the local man, the inside connection, who had worked with Donetti and then very probably killed him? O'Rourke? A possibility. But the skinny guy just didn't seem bad enough to me. I guess maybe a trained cop would say that didn't make any difference. Maybe so. Then there was my personal choice, Ford Messner. Something about that guy... Except Gina gave him a perfect alibi for the time of Carla Teacher's death. Which, according to French, eliminated him from Donetti's shove, too.

Lots of possibilities. God-damn pimp. Is that what the murdered man had said? Well, that opened a lot of doors. Condi Capucho, with the unlikely name and a passion for guns. Mickey System, a professional rube who'd steal the collection plate at a Sunday church service. Paul Carter, who maybe wasn't a pimp, strictly speaking. But he had the background for a push like this. Jack Kilgallen? No chance. The kid was too dumb and too salty. What I'd seen of Marino, he wouldn't have picked a no-talent like Kilgallen for a partner.

The kid came back. He had a tall drink in his hand which he handed me in exchange for his game.

Dan greeted me wearily. "Hi, Johnny. Boy, you should have been here tonight."

"I'm here now. Take a break."

The girls looked up, went back to work. Fran brushed the back of her hand over her eyes, droned the words of the game.

I ran Dan off, said to Bev, "Take a break. I'll take the payoff on both sides."

"You can't, Johnny." Fran said. "We're too busy."

I just looked at her. I had no words. The soft skin of her face glowed in the indirect lighting; there was no sign of a bruise or discoloration where I'd slapped her. But I could see one. And it stopped my tongue. I just shook my head, glad suddenly to be able to stand next to her, look at her, appreciate the cool womanliness.

Bev said, "Okay, boss," and squirmed out of the crush. Fran and I worked the layout and I had to call upon all of my experience, use all the tricks learned in twenty years of shuffling chips and watching dice, to keep up with the game.

I studied Fran. When she wasn't looking. When she reached out over the table to hook the dice, the firm line of hip and thigh, breast and arm made the blood climb in my head.

"Comes go, Mr. Berlin," she said.

I flushed and moved chips around. She looked up, met my gaze levelly; her eyes were dark with liquid movement under the surface. The pale hair was flipped forward around clean features and the white collar of her dress kicked highlights up under the sweeping neck curve, firm underjaw.

"It's all right, Johnny," she said, so that only I could hear. "It's all right."

But it wasn't. And we both knew it.

We ran out of action at three-thirty. In atonement for having been late, I'd worked straight through. Fran had, too. She wouldn't quit and I realized it was something she had to do, so I didn't insist. She was dead tired when we quit.

The big room was empty save for Dan and Condi when I carried the box out to make the count. The chairs and tables were scattered in a garish clutter; all lights had been turned off save the neon stripping behind the bar.

I was tired. Accumulation of wearies. I swung a leg over a stool, dumped the box on the hardwood.

The phone rang. It is very quiet in Edson at four in the morning. And doubly so in an empty night club. The clatter was enormous. I came awake first, reached over the bar, pulled the instrument to the wood.

"Cherbourg. Johnny Berlin."

"Johnny, listen," a woman's voice said. "I'm glad I finally got you. Johnny, I'm scared. They're crazy. It's out of hand and I'm afraid."

"Wait," I said. My hand gripped the phone so hard it hurt. "Sheila? Is that you?"

"Yes, yes! Listen. I had to sneak off…"

Her voice trailed off. I shouted into the phone.

"Sheila! Sheila, what's wrong?"

Her loud breathing came into my ear. Then she said, "I had to stop. Mops came by. You've got to get me out of here! You've—"

"Where are you? I'll be there as quick as possible."

"Oh, Johnny, hurry! I'll tell you—Don't!" There was a loud noise on the line, then a muffled scream. The phone buzzed emptily on the drum of my ear while I shouted like a crazy man into the mouthpiece at my end.

Then very softly the connection was broken.

I pressed down, still holding the phone to my ear. The operator came on and I asked for Police Headquarters.

"What is it, Johnny?" Dan asked. "Can I help?"

I waved him to silence, got French's home phone from the desk sergeant. Then I hung up, sat there for a minute thinking. Sheila was in danger. From whom, I didn't know. Unless that slip about Mops—obviously Mops Parisi, the ape I'd cut—meant anything. In which case it meant O'Rourke. Which meant the joint down the beach road.

"Dan, I gotta go."

Fran met me at the door.

"Johnny, where are you going?"

The girl stepped close to me, gripped the lapels of my coat. Her face was white in the near-gloom of the alcove.

"I've got something to do. Call this number till you get George French. Tell him I had Sheila on the phone. She was cut off. Chances are pretty good that she's being held somewhere against her will. He's got to start looking."

"Where, Johnny?"

I took Fran's slim wrists, set her aside. "I don't know. Just get him and tell him and that's all you can do. May damn well be all anyone can do."

Fran moved against me then and for one time-stopped moment we were closer than we'd ever been. She kissed my mouth, but it was hard and it stayed that way. She stepped back.

"All right, Johnny, Do what you have to do. But I'm going along. Dan can call George French."

"No," I said. "You can't." But she had already gone to find Gurion.

I walked rapidly out into the swirling mist of the early morning. The road was wet; the cars were covered with moisture, windows speckled with fog. I heard Fran running behind me.

"Go home," I told her, pushed her to the little car.

She didn't resist. But her chin jutted. She climbed into her car, rolled down the window.

"This is just like the first time," I said. "Remember?"

"I remember. Johnny, take me with you."

"No."

"Then I'll follow," she said, and began rolling up the glass.

"Wait. All right. We'll go in your car. But you'd better know this. If we find what I expect, there may be trouble."

Her eyes closed; hands tightened on the wheel. Then she nodded, opened her eyes and they were clear violet and soft as purple down.

"All right. Let's go."

I got in, swung to face her on the seat while she got the engine started. She glanced at me, face carefully controlled.

"Where to?"

"Across the street. The motel. Stop in front of Condi's place. You know which one it is?"

"Yes." She whipped the coupe out of the lot backwards, stopped it and sent it screaming over the fog-wet road to the motel driveway. "What for, Johnny? What are you stopping here for?"

"I need a gun," I said.

CHAPTER FIFTEEN

Condi gave me a gun. A Luger in fine shape, loaded deadly—
eight in the clip and one in the chamber. He wanted to come
along. But I left him there in the two-room cabin, polishing his collection, and drove through the road-hugging fog to Coley's Club.

I hit the place like an assault wave. Fran swooped into the
drive and I hit the clay running. By the time I got to the back
door I was moving like a seatback in the clear. The door slammed
off its hinges, banged against the wall.

I stood there, gun in hand. There wasn't a sound. This was
the office where O'Rourke had made his threatening pitch. I
saw the leather couch in the gloom; Parisi's blood probably still
stained it. But there was nobody home.

The hall door was open. I went through, stuck my head in
every door, investigated every room. Nobody. The bar was dark
and empty; the fireplace was cold and had no fire laid in it. I
grabbed a bottle off the bar and hotfooted it back to the car.

Fran's eyes were enormous in the darkness of the front seat.
She started the engine as I slid in beside her.

"Nothing, Johnny?"

"Not a damn thing." I leaned back against the seat. The motor
idled, puffing clouds of vapor into the fog. Fran sat quietly, waiting for me to tell her where to go. "I don't know," I said finally.

Then, "Downtown, Police headquarters. I want to talk to
French."

I twisted on the seat, watched Fran as she drove. She did it
efficiently, only now and then sparing a glance from the road for

me. She was beautiful. And not cold. Different from the women I'd known and therefore hard for me to understand. But not cold. I must have been walking through life with my head down. Sometimes you can't see for looking.

"Fran," I said.

"Yes?" She turned, flicked a small smile, then paid attention once more to the road. "What is it, Johnny?"

"You know what I'm doing? You got any idea what it means that I'm knocking myself out like this?"

She nodded. "I know. You told me about the rule. Mind your own business, tend to your own hustle. Never rank the other man's play." Her tongue ran over red lips. She smiled sadly. "I know, all right. And I know what it means now that you've found out you're capable of feeling for someone other than Johnny Berlin."

"Maybe." I sucked my cigarette, threw the end out the wind-wing into the rushing morning air. "But I'm breaking a lifetime rule. And it comes hard, Fran. But that kid. That kid ..."

"I know, darling. I know."

She slowed to a stop in front of the police station. I slid across the seat, put my arms around her. My head nudged hers around and I looked into those wonderful eyes, inches from mine.

I said, "Say it again."

Her arms crept slowly from between us, slid around me. "Darling," she said and closed her eyes. "Darling, darling ..."

Her lips opened and I touched them almost fearfully. It was a clumsy kiss, moist and inexperienced. But it shook us both because of the promise, the hint of wild sweetness to come.

"This isn't the time," I whispered. "But it won't be long."

"Yes, Johnny." She buried her head on my shoulder, moved it from side to side. "Oh, I was wrong, darling. I want you. And I'll take you any way you say. Any way at all. That's the way it was meant to be."

"No," I said. "Your rules are the right ones. I never played by them before, but I'm game. I love you, Fran."

She started to cry. Her body softened under my hands and I knew I had to send her home or ruin the cleanest thing that had ever happened to me.

"Go home and go to sleep now. I'll call you when I can."

I put a hand on the beautiful blonde hair, rumpled it tenderly. Her eyes came up, filled with tears. She smiled, sniffled.

"Yes, Johnny."

I kissed her quickly, climbed out into the strengthening light.

"One of these days I'll get some sleep," I said.

Her face stuck out of the window on the driver's side when I'd walked around. She stretched out a hand.

"Johnny, be careful. Please?"

I shifted the gun down between my belt and my belly. The grimness settled again, chasing elation

"Yeah, sure." I held her hand, rubbed the back of it with my thumb. "Good night, Fran. Or should it be good morning?"

She pulled me, grabbed my tie and touched my lips briefly with hers. Warm velvet and a cool promise.

"There'll be a thousand good mornings," she breathed.

French wasn't there. The rookie cop I'd come to know during the Donetti mess was on duty. He gave me coffee, but no information.

"All I know," he said, "is the lieutenant tore out of here after a phone call from your boss."

"Dan called then. Where'd he go? How many men did he take?"

The kid shrugged wide blue shoulders. "Dunno, Johnny. I didn't see him go. I know he said something about a boat Messner owns."

I walked down Third Street to Main and the Kenyon Hotel corner. My eyes ached. It would have been simple to walk into the lobby, ride up in the creaky elevator and fall into my bed and forget everything. Everything but what I'd found with Fran. It would be nice to savor that, roll it around on my mind. What did

I owe Carla Teacher? Maybe nothing. Maybe more than I could repay with a simple act of revenge. And that's what I pursued now. Revenge. Raw and green and as senseless as the greed that had started the whole vicious mess.

It seemed I spent half my life watching McKaneville awaken. Traffic was picking up. Mill workers on the way to Wood Town. I admitted to myself that I wasn't going to help anyone running around in the dark. What did I think I could do for Sheila with no idea where she was? French was on the job. He'd check the known places.

There were several things I could do, still stumbling. See Paul Carter. He was still eligible. Find Messner. That I'd like to do, but I didn't know where to start. Or could I act sensible and leave it to the police?

"Where the hell you been, man? You sure are a hard fella to find."

I stopped. I'd walked into the lobby, started across toward the elevator. Mickey System rose up out of one of the high-backed chairs, confronted me.

"Here I am," I said. "What do you want?"

"You look beat." He folded the paper he'd been reading, threw it behind him to the chair. "Let's get some coffee. I got something to tell you."

We went to the Sweet Shop next door. In a booth, with fumes rising from cups of hot, fresh coffee, Mickey smiled wearily across the linoleum-topped table.

"You got bags under your eyes, man," he said. "Smoke?"

I took a cigarette, held a light for the little hustler. He sucked a mouthful of smoke, held it, looked at me.

"I'm beginning to wish I'd leveled with you in the beginning," he said.

"What do you mean, Mickey?" I flipped the match, stirred some of the heat from my coffee absently. "If you've got something to tell me, get to it. I'm tired and I'm evil."

"I can see that. What happened?"

I sighed. "I got a call from Sheila. She was in trouble. I took off like a big-assed bird to save the mortgage and wound up riding around wondering what the hell I thought I was doing. So it don't feel good. Mostly because she really might be in trouble."

Mickey studied me through the smoke. He lifted his cup. "She is," he said, and sipped.

"She is? You sound like you know something. Let's have it."

He nodded. "I got a whisper through my old lady, Toni. You don't know her, but you will pretty soon. She works in a joint in Welles. Marti Thayer's."

I expected him to be apologetic or something about the fact that his wife was a hustler. But he wasn't. Then I thought how silly it was that a man who had fractured most of the moral laws should draw lines, and split hairs and judge others.

"Why are you telling me now?"

He dropped his smoking butt into the saucer, watched it sizzle in the spilled coffee. "I dunno. Why are you messing in the thing?"

"I got run off the road, remember?"

"Yeah. Well, maybe it's the way that kid got it. I'm a hustler and pimp, maybe, but that's too much, you know?" He shrugged his shoulders impatiently. "Anyway, what's the difference? I don't want the syndicate. I'd have to leave. And I like this country."

"I know where Sheila is," Mickey said. "Maybe she can help you. I called Toni, like I do regular, and when she told me the redhead was there, I tried to find you."

"You mean she's at this—what was the name of that place?"

"Marti Thayer's. It's the old Commercial Hotel in Welles. Toni says Mops Parisi brought the broad and had her locked up in a room. And that's all I know, man."

"It might be plenty, Mickey. I got to get out there. I don't know what I'll do, but I got to talk to that girl."

He reached in a side pocket, got a small ring of keys. They hit the table, slid to my hand.

"Take my car. It's the new Buick right around back. Black one. Say hello to Toni for me. And Johnny..."

I'd gotten up, started to struggle into my coat. "Yes?"

"Remember Toni, will you, if a hassle starts?"

I thought of the gun nestling against my belly. And of two bodies already cold and nothing to lose for whoever had made them that way.

"I will, Mick. Thanks. You're a good man."

"I'm outa my skull," he said. "But lotsa luck."

The Buick was new and it would go. I poured it over the road much too fast until I realized that nothing would be gained by killing myself. Plus the fact that it had been hours since Sheila's call. If anything was going to happen to her it would have been accomplished by now. I slowed, fiddled with the radio knob, got some early-morning music, settled more comfortably into the seat. Welles was thirty-some miles.

The road was snaky and the morning was becoming clear and sunny. Spots of dampness showed where the sun hadn't reached, filtered as it was through foliage. I rolled the window partway down, let the air blow into my face. Keep me awake. When I got to Welles I'd have something else to do. Try to stay alive.

Halfway there I stopped at a roadside diner, went inside and called the Devil's Play Spot. Gilbertson wasn't there. Or if he was, I couldn't get him. I got a sleepy Gina and listened patiently to an astonishing vocabulary of cuss words before I could get a word in.

"Okay," I said, when she paused for breath. "I'm sorry I told you that. I was messed up. That kid's death threw me a little. And I had to go to the club."

"You could have been more subtle, darling." Her voice grew husky, now that her anger was gone. "After all, it isn't as if we weren't ... friends."

"I'm not sure we were ever friends. But let that go. Listen, I want you to do something for me and it might be damned important, so don't goof."

"Of course, Johnny. What is it?"

"Get hold of Gilbertson. Tell him I found the girl."

"Found the girl? Found what girl? Johnny, are you still messing in that thing?" Her voice climbed. "Haven't I told you to mind your own business before you get hurt?"

"Hey, look, I'm not asking you."

The line buzzed. Then she said, "All right. What's the message?"

"That's better. Tell good old Horace I may need him and his Commandos. I'm on my way right now to a—well, a joint in Welles. Marti Thayer's. Got that?"

"Of course, it's a notorious bawdy house. What—"

"Bawdy house. That's the word. Tell him to get there quick unless I call and tell him not to. Okay?"

"Johnny, listen. You're going to get hurt. You're messing where you have no business. Now—"

"Will you do it or won't you?"

"All right!" she blazed. "But I hope you get your pretty head caved in! Go on. Go to your whore house. Maybe you'll get some ideas."

I put my mouth close to the mouthpiece, made a kissing sound with my lips.

"None you wouldn't recognize, baby."

I stood outside and let the sun hit my face for a minute. It felt good. For a little while I forgot the mounting tensions, the half-warped surges inside me. I thought about Gina. She was a bomb. And no doubt she would be very loving if I should take Gilbertson's offer to manage the resort. Right then I wondered if I hadn't been hasty in turning down the deal.

CHAPTER SIXTEEN

The Buick got me to Welles in a matter of minutes and I found the hotel that housed the Thayer nautchery. It wasn't Polly Adler's. An orange crate with windows, two stories high, with a bare, wood stairway reaching up from the alley to a tiny porch perched against the building's rear. Steep and rickety with one handrail. I parked the Buick down the alley and walked back. The stairway looked like the ladder to a high wire. I went up, noticing a yellow Cadillac parked across from the steps.

A colored maid gave me a light hassle, but I pushed in, stood for a minute in the early morning gloom. I was in a long corridor spaced with doors on either side. There was a single bulb halfway down and a window at the far end, about a mile and a half away.

The maid said, "Sir, Miz Thayer ain't doin' no receivin' this—"

"She's receiving. Shut the door and disappear."

Dark tunnel with doors. I didn't feel good about this at all. My hand found the Luger, loosened it in my belt. Radio music was loud from somewhere. Fans of light hit the worn carpeting from under several doors. The girls, I guessed. A heavy odor hung in the air. Sweet, but a little too sweet. Like a dissolute debutante breathing alcohol through a fog of Chanel Number Five.

The single bulb was in front of the kitchen and that's where I went. The door was open. One blowzy woman drinking coffee under a window; music from a chrome radio, much too loud now that I was near it. The kitchen was bright, like an advertisement.

"What the hell do you want, mac?"

I said nothing, stepped in and looked around.

She raised her voice over the radio. "You hear me, Elmer? We're closed."

This, I thought, is the fabulous Marti Thayer. Years ago, maybe. Not now. Too many hard years. A pudgy bottle-blonde with sagging breast pushing at a cerise wrapper and hard eyes in a doll's face. Her voice had some of the quality of a saw ripping hardwood.

"You don't know me, Marti," I said. "But I know you. And I know you got a redhead named Sheila here somewhere. I want to see her. That's all. Then I go. No trouble, no scuffle, no noise."

I had to say it loud. Damn radio. Her eyes held mine for a moment, then slid away over my shoulder. A small chill chased over me. What the hell was this?

I stepped away from the door, looked around again. Still just a kitchen. The corridor was empty, too. Back to the woman, the feeling growing in me.

"It's nine o'clock," I said.

"So what do you want from me? An endorsement? We got nobody named Sheila, never had nobody by that name. Now get out before you get hurt."

"Little early for you to be up, isn't it?"

She glowered at me, grabbed a bottle from the table and poured a healthy slug into her coffee. Something was sure as hell wrong. No whorehouse in the world opens at nine in the morning. Marti Thayer was not only up, she was agitated. She gulped a shot of the coffee royale, whirled.

"Didn't you hear me, creep? Get the hell out."

"Very good," I said. "You almost make me believe you don't know me, have no idea why I'm here. Well, cut the crap. I want Sheila and I'll see her if I have to break down every door in the joint."

The woman lifted her doll face; the eyes were venomous. She opened her mouth and screamed, "Frank!"

I slapped her. She slammed her cup down, breaking the saucer. Her eyes were like flat metal discs.

"Oh, you're paid for, you are," she said. "You're dead, Berlin. Now you get your head changed."

"You said my name."

"All right!" she blazed. "So I know who you are. Sure I know who you are. Mops Parisi came here with his belly out and his arm slashed a week ago. I know you're messing in something that's too big for you."

"Tell me about Sheila," I said.

But she didn't get a chance to tell me about anything. I heard a step, tried to turn, reaching for the Luger. All I got was a flash impression of a husky figure in a black leather jacket and then I was pushing up the floor from where his clubbed gun had put me. My head spun. I reached for a chrome chair leg, jerked at the thing and it whirled around me, hit the kid at the knees.

He stumbled back and I saw a confused young face, knobby with rage. He had a handful of blue automatic. The snout lifted as he stumbled back. There wasn't time to do anything but push. I pushed. I pushed like hell.

He struck the refrigerator, bounced toward me swinging the gun. I ducked, still on only one knee, took his body over my shoulder. He hit me on the back with the gun, but I squeezed and he came down with me on the linoleum.

Marti was shouting something. I was too busy to listen to her. The kid was strong as a bull. He kept trying to feed me that damn gun and finally I got his wrist in my hand, held it out wide.

Marti screamed, "Hold him, lover! Give them time to get out ..."

And the kid heaved under me. He was like a bag full of muscles, all snapping. He was trying, but I had the gun hand and I wasn't about to let it go. He whacked me here and there. But he didn't shoot me and at the time that seemed to be the thing to avoid. Finally I got him turned, straddled him, slammed my right hand into his twisted face. If he hit me after that I didn't feel it. Maybe I went a little crazy. I grabbed with both hands, jacket and hair, and beat his head on the floor. The gun went flying. We heaved up together, me holding on like grim death. He tried to butt me and I ran my shoe sole down his shinbone, stepped back. He bent with pain and I hit him in the mouth. He started down and I swung my foot into his gut.

He fell like a sack of Jello.

There was a lot of yelling. My ears and eyes were working, but not together. Several girls in all stages of undress milled around the door.

Then I remembered what the Thayer woman had said. Give them time, she'd said. And now she was gone. I busted through the doorway, scattering screaming females.

Marti Thayer stood at the end of the hall peering out of one of the skinny windows that flanked the door. I got there at a dead run, jerked the fat madam aside.

She hollered, "Frank!"

But I had the window. I saw what it was that interested her in the alley below. Sheila, the long-stemmed redhead, was being forced into the yellow Cadillac across the alley. I had a clear shot of Mops Parisi, one arm in a sling, pushing the girl into the front seat. She was fully dressed in a green tailored suit and carried a large traveling bag. Her hair was a sullen flame in the morning sun.

I reached for the door handle and Marti Thayer landed in the middle of my back. Flailing arms stunned me before I could turn enough in the narrow hall to grab the raging woman. Christ, she was slippery in that silk wrapper!

As I struggled with her, over her shoulder I saw the leather-jacketed kid stumbling up the hall. He was bent and humped, but he had the gun clutched in one hand. My own

Luger was gone.

Hooked fingers raked at my eyes. I got one wrist, twisted sharply. I didn't want to hit the broad, but I was going to have to do something. Then she dropped her head forward, smashed hard frontal bone against my nose.

Tears spurted. Technicolor. A silk-slimy leg slid between mine and she lifted her knee. I squeezed my thighs together to keep from getting split to my breastbone and got my hand under her chin. My hips braced against one wall, I surged and shoved hard. Marti popped out of my grasp, hit the other wall. Her robe fell open. I drove a fist short and hard into the soft flesh below her navel.

She hit the floor, sliding down the wall.

But it had taken too long. The kid came the last few feet like the Los Angeles Rams. This time when he clubbed his gun my head was right there. He hit me twice and only the fact that he still felt the effects of my boot in the belly kept him from tearing my head off. Still he almost put me out.

He did put me down. And I grabbed a leg, pulled. He came down swinging. I was spending a hell of a lot of time on the floor with this guy. But here I could nullify the effect of that damn gun—if he didn't bury it in my head first.

We both grunted and busted each other almost silly. He gave out first; I didn't hit him extra hard or anything. He just got full first. He sagged. Then slumped. I got to my knees and it was like climbing Mount Everest.

I could see his face down there. I raised a fist that weighed twenty-seven pounds, dropped it onto the kid's jaw. It landed and I fell with the blow.

Couldn't just lay there. That would be real stupid. Get up, Berlin. Get up and scoot and go find Sheila.

I got up somehow. And I got the door open, ignoring the chatter of the hallway full of girls.

Then I was alone on the postage-stamp-sized porch in the uncompromising sunlight. My eyes burned. I turned carefully toward the stairs. I hurt here and there, but it didn't register, really. Later the tooth I could feel sticking into my lip would give me hell. Right now it was a single instrument in a symphony orchestra. I put a hand on the building, steadied myself. Better get to the God-damn car on the double.

I found the hand rail, gripped it. The steps seemed to lead downward interminably. I took the first step. There's always a first step and I took it. Boy, I took it!

And it was a dandy.

I hit once, halfway down and felt nothing at all after that. Not even the concrete at the bottom.

One step took me thirty-five miles. To a starched bed in a bare room, everything white and clean.

CHAPTER SEVENTEEN

I came awake slowly and I knew right away where I was. A hospital room. Detective, that's me. Everything was white including the blinds on the windows facing the bed I was lying on. And a stocky figure in starched white stood beside me. She said something. I didn't catch it. I was cataloguing hurts; trying to see if I was all there.

"You have visitors, Mr. Berlin."

I turned my eyes and they both worked. Some. Still fuzzy and red, but they worked.

I cleared my throat. "Visitors? Me?"

She nodded. Now I could see her. She had a clear-skinned, ruddy face with ordinary features; not pretty, not plain. The cap perched on top of a growth of fine, dark hair.

"Sure. One of them's been here ever since you came." She smiled, eyes lighting. "The pretty blonde."

"Where is here?"

"Here is the McKaneville Medical Center. And I'm Miss Holmberg."

I grinned, felt stitches pulling. "Howdy. I'm King Farouk."

"Too skinny," she said.

"Skinny?" I raised up in outrage and almost left this world.

"Here, Mr. Berlin. You be good."

She caught me, helped me sit up. I couldn't lift my left arm. Mostly because it had about a ton of plaster wrapped around it. I had bruises everywhere. I ran my right hand over my face, feeling, probing, while Miss Holmberg cranked my bed up. Not too bad. Couple of stitches in the cheek, around the mouth. A fine mouse on one eye; a small patch, grainy with clotting powder, on my head.

"Anything else besides the arm?" I asked.

"No bones, if that's what you mean. But you have the most magnificent collection of bruises I've ever seen."

"Oh, you've been looking, huh?"

I ran my good arm under the covers; I was right. A shorty gown and nothing else.

Miss Holmberg blushed. She rustled to the table by the bed-side, lit a cigarette for me.

"I'm a nurse," she said primly.

"I'm glad," I said.

Then she smiled, shook her head. "No wonder all the women."

I took a drag of the Camel, almost died with pleasure as the smoke found the long-denied passages. It made me giddy, though. Women, she'd said.

"Oh, boy, women," the nurse said, leering. "Not counting the blonde—" She ticked off fingers. "—one brunette with an abso-lutely illegal figure. Another wearing slacks."

"Who's here now?"

"The blonde."

"Her name's Fran."

"And a policeman. The others have been in and out."

I sighed. "Since when?"

"Since yesterday noon when you came in from Welles in the ambulance."

"Yesterday, huh? What time is it now?"

She glanced at a lapel watch. "Five-thirty."

"How long do I have to stay?"

"Doctor says a few days. For observation. You're all fixed up, but, boy, can you sleep!"

"Yeah." I moved. Felt all right. I pushed the cigarette into the ashtray, ran the fingers of my right hand through my hair. "Let 'em in."

Better get it done. Because now I was remembering all the things I'd been unable to do and what might have happened during my blackout. And something else. Something I couldn't for the damnedest trying pull into the light of memory. Important, too. Something about Sheila. A little thing.

Fran came in and the room got lighter. Her face was drawn with strain, but she looked wonderful. A tight, hip-hugging dress, black and simply cut; a tiny box perching on the creamy hair.

"Hi," she said.

George French followed her in; both walked to the bed. I nodded. I couldn't say a word.

Fran's eyes misted and she broke finally.

"Oh, Johnny," she said, and fell on me, almost ruining me. "You crazy, crazy darling!"

"Hey," I squeaked. "Watch the grip, kid."

She pulled back, lips trembling. Then she kissed me very tenderly on my battered lips, got up and went to the window to repair her make-up and her composure.

"Hi, George."

"Hello, Johnny. You're lucky."

My face burned. I remembered that Fran had been his girl and, for the first time in my life, I cared about a thing like that. No reason, but it was there.

"You look beat," the lieutenant said, straddling the hard chair by the bed.

"Am beat. And you look tired, George. Real tired. What's the pitch?"

"We didn't get 'em, Johnny. Wait, before you flip. Mickey called me. We made time from here to Welles. I knew better than to call that vegetable that runs the police force there in

Welles. He's in Marti's pocket. And her bed, too, the story goes. Anyway—"

"What you're trying to say is, they got away."

He nodded. "All right. So I'm a bum cop. But you tell me how I should know they shouldn't be allowed to leave? The girls didn't tell me. They don't like to talk to cops. All I knew for sure was you'd been there, made trouble and got bounced."

"Boy, I got bounced." I reached for a cigarette, couldn't make it across my body. "Light me one, huh?"

"Sure. So Frank and Marti scrammed. Here." He handed me the cigarette, lit one for himself. "Toni, that girl of Mickey's, finally told me a little of the pitch. Enough to put out an APB for Mops Parisi and Sheila and to pick up Coley O'Rourke."

"O'Rourke? Then it is cleaned up. He's got to be it. Parisi's his goon. He's—"

I stopped. French nodded, slab face relaxing a bit. "You came to it, too, huh? So did I. He's alibied but real stinking good for the Teacher bit. And as good as anybody for the other. We shook down his joint, found nothing. His house, too. I know only that he's scared. And I couldn't find out why."

"You run into Gilbertson yet?"

He nodded, mouth twisting sourly. "Yeah. We took a run out with the sheriff's investigator from the DA's office. The guy's clean. All around. Except for that mess he controls out there."

"If he finds out who did it, you'll never try the man, you know."

"I know." His knuckles cracked loudly. "Well, I've got to get back to work. Marti and that guy took off in the Cad with a box-ful of money they got from a safety deposit vault. No trace so far. But they'll show somewhere."

"Sure," I said. "And when they do, you're home free. But what about Sheila?"

He got up slowly, face hardening. "Sheila. If she'd come to us in the first place..." He got his brown felt off the table, pushed it on the back of his head. "But she didn't. And I'm afraid for her, Johnny."

"So am I. Where's Ford Messner?"

"I ran him down yesterday. He's living on his boat around the Bay curve at a place called Bowldersville. A wide spot. Fishing village. He's still clean so far as we know. He wouldn't say a word about Sheila except that he was worried about her, hadn't seen her."

"I still like him as a suspect," I said. I threw my cigarette end to the immaculate floor. "I like him real good."

"So do I. But we can't shake Gina Donetti's alibi for the time the Teacher kid got it." He walked to the door. "If you remember anything, Johnny, let me know I'm going to make a fast check on Marti Thayer and Frank."

"All right, George."

His eyes turned to Fran, still at the window waiting for us to be finished. His mouth tightened and he looked at me, eyes narrowing to a perfectly obvious threat.

"You be good," he growled. "You're lucky, but you ain't good."

"I'm trying, George."

Fran spun, saw the play. French pulled his hat down, stretched his heavy shoulders.

"Maybe you are, slicker. Maybe you are, at that."

He left. And Miss Holmberg came in, stuck me with another needle.

Fran smiled when we were alone again. "Hi, anyway," she said in a small voice. Her lips stayed curved and her breasts rose and fell very nicely with the unevenness of her breathing.

"Come here," I said, pulling her to me. "I'm tired of being beat up. I'd like to be kissed for a change."

"Wait," she said. "I have a couple of things I'm supposed to tell you. Dan isn't here because he's got to open and run the place tonight. Same with Bev. She really wanted to come. And Dan has a proposition for you." She looked away, pulled her hand free. "If you want to stay around here, that is."

I took her hand again. "Tell," I said. "Never mind the commercial. You'll oversell your product."

She smiled; her lips looked so much better curved. And there was no line between her eyes. All smooth. I could see a pulse moving under the creamy skin of her neck.

"A deal to run the Cherbourg," she said, in a rush. "Everything, the works. With a conditional payment and then alternate divisions to him and his wife and kids on a lease with option to buy."

I pulled her down, kissed her till the bruises sang out in protest. Then I let her go. I put my hand on her hip, looked up at her.

"I'll think about it, woman. Not jumping anymore?"

She busied herself with the little hat. Her face flamed. Then her eyes narrowed; the violet turning to smoky blue. "You're lucky you're sick," she whispered and ran lightly to the door.

I kept thinking about Sheila. You don't learn many prayers around carnivals and gambling joints. But I figured this was a good time to make one up and I played it by ear.

The doctor came and went. While he was there changing bandages and telling me I couldn't leave for at least three days, Gilbertson came with Marc. I brought them up to date, suggested they get on finding Parisi before the big ape had time to get the redhead clear out of the country.

"I shall do that of course, Johnny," Gilbertson said. "Perhaps we can turn up something. Also the Thayer woman and her escort. The circles they run in are not unknown to me. And some of my associates."

"You better make it quick with Sheila," I said. "But I'm afraid it's too late."

"What do you think?"

"I think maybe we'll find her some cold, foggy morning drifting with the shavings and garbage off the end of that point out past the Kilgore Hills. That's what I think." My face tightened, I made a fist and looked at it steadily. "And it's my fault, probably. If I'd kept my nose out, she might have been all right."

"Perhaps," the banker said. He smoothed his gray lapels. "But not likely. She knew something damaging. I wish I knew what."

We left it there and he left with the big-nosed Marc, promising to return.

I got out of bed, found my clothes in the closet. They were a real mess. No underwear. I put the pants on, tucked in the hospital shorty. Shoes without socks. The shirt was stiff with blood so I passed it. My coat—second-best suit coat—was pretty bad. I brushed it clumsily, still not able to navigate too well. The cast bothered me, too. But I got the coat on finally, exhausted by the effort. I'd had to slit the left sleeve clear up to allow passage of the elbow-to-knuckles cast.

But I was dressed. The table drawer yielded a wadded and stiff bundle of money, keys for nothing and my wallet. I stuffed the junk in my pockets, picked up the cigarettes and made for the corridor.

Miss Holmberg, sitting alone at the street door, a tiny light shedding illumination for the racks of charts, looked up as I stumbled toward her.

"Mr. Berlin!" She rose, hurried around the desk. "You can't. You should be in bed Sit here while I get help."

I gritted my teeth. "You sit me there, *you'll* need help. Get out of my way."

"Mr. Berlin ..."

"You want to help, Holmberg? Then get me a drink. A big belt. Something to start my motor running."

She looked at me for a long moment, eyes drawn in a frown. Then she nodded, took off through a door behind the desk. She was back in a minute with a beaker half-full of medicinal alcohol in an ounce of orange juice.

I got it down. And it almost knocked me down. But soon I could feel the warmth, the flowing strength. I winked my best eye at the nurse.

"Thanks, Holmberg."

Something glinted in her eyes; a silver drop of pity. Or maybe admiration.

"Go ahead," she said. "I hope you break your neck."

But I didn't. I got outside and it was a beautiful night. Soft-dark and warm with no chilling wind or fog from the treacherous sea. The clinic was on the south end of town between Main Street and Kilgore. I should have called a cab. Traffic flowing by a block away drew me and I started off in that direction.

Car lights swept around the corner, pinned me, then roared down in my direction. I felt fear for a moment, then saw that the car was stopping, slewing from side to side as brakes were applied. The heavy machine rocked to a halt beside me.

Mickey System piled out, leaving the door open.

"Johnny," the little hustler cried. "I was coming to get you."

"Mickey. I'm glad to see you, man. Let's—"

"Get in," he said, taking my arm. "We got things to do."

Mickey jumped in, threw the Buick in gear and raced past the hospital, turned onto Kilgore, scattering cars and leaving horns blowing in our wake. The car straightened and the little dice man looked out over the wheel, face tight with concentration.

"What's happening?" I asked, over the motor's howl. "Where we going?"

"Sheila's place. I found her."

"You found her." I sat up, tried to get oriented. "You mean Sheila's all right? She's—"

I stopped. His face told me. Mickey looked ahead, chin raised, apple cheeks pushed up.

"I went by the house on the way up to see you just now," he said. "Sheila's place, in the Hills. Just before I got there a car pulled out of the drive, speeded away without lights. I stopped and looked in the front window."

He turned, eyes shadowed in the yellow dash light.

"She's dead, Johnny."

CHAPTER EIGHTEEN

I didn't hurt anymore. The Buick howled up Kilgore to the Hills, circled around the top to Crescenta. Nobody spoke. There was nothing to say. My cast lay in my lap, bumping as we rode; the aches in my bruised body had retreated behind the undefined burn that was building in me, bubbling and hardening my face, pouring energy back into drained tissue.

We pulled into the weed-grown drive and I got out alone.

"Stay here."

"Johnny, you better—"

"Stay here until I get in, anyway."

The porch had been cleared of its clutter. The front door, squares of thick glass in wood frames, was closed and locked. I tried to peer through, could see nothing. I touched the small window next to the knob with my good hand, drew back the cast and slammed it through the glass.

Not very neat, but I was in. Glass crunched under my feet. The entrance hall was dark. I felt for light switches, found none and kept going. The living room opened off to the left. I stopped just outside the door, listened intently. Nothing. Nothing but the ordinary night sounds; wind softly working on the wires outside, the faint mutter of the Buick's engine.

She was there. On the floor next to the spindle-legged writing desk. Her long legs were folded and wrapped with what looked like wire. Her arms had been crossed tight over her breasts and bound that way. Her face was turned away.

I took a deep breath, was glad when it hurt inside. Then I walked forward, trying to look everywhere. A faint light from the high moon shone in the side window; a slant of it struck Sheila's face. Her lips were drawn back, an expression of horror marring the sulky beauty of her features. There was a large bruise on one eye; a cut, dried and at least a day old, on her upper lip. The eyes were wide open.

I was tight. Wound like a dollar watch. My right hand fumbled, found a large standard lamp. I squeezed it. After a moment, I was all right. My belly cooled, seemed to grow tight.

"The dirty bastards!"

I kept saying it. It was silly, but I couldn't stop. The wall switch was handy; I flipped it. Soft lights sprang from all sides.

The room hadn't been mussed. No struggle. Sheila's body lay on its side and I still didn't know why she'd died. I moved to it, rolled it on its back. I saw the weights. Sash weights, new and ugly, attached to the ropes that bound the girl.

Steps on the porch. Mickey came in and it wasn't so bad any more.

"Jesus Christ!" Mickey said. His cherub's face was old in the artificial light, lined and sick. He moved to the body, knelt.

"What killed her?" It was my voice, but it had an echo-chamber effect in my head.

He looked up. "Knife," he said. "Through the left breast. Real thin one. She bled, but her arms cover it."

"She might have bled, but she didn't do it here."

Mickey stood quickly, lit a cigarette with trembling fingers. He puffed out smoke. "How do you know?"

I pointed to the corpse's feet. The shoes were black suede, thin soles with high, spiked heels.

"Wet. Look at her feet. And the curve of the instep is clotted with mud. Take a look at it."

He did.

Mickey said, "Not loam, like the woods. It's red clay, Johnny."

It all began dropping into place in my mind. I knew the whole bit. Well, almost all. It had to be Ford Messner. He was Donetti's double-crossing partner.

"Any ground like that around Bowldersville?" I asked.

Mickey straightened, brushed off his hands. "No, but there is around Coley's Club. The parking lot, anyway. Messner, huh?"

"Messner," I said. "How'd you know?"

He shrugged. "Doesn't take a detective. Weights tied on her. Messner's old lady and she was anxious to tell somebody something. Somebody other than Messner. So he pushes her. He has a boat."

"Why would they bring her here from the club? Why not right onto the boat?"

"Well," said Mickey. "Ford's boat is a twenty-four footer. Cabin cruiser called the *Blue Chip*. He can bring it down the channel right past the bottom of this hill. Maybe they changed their minds about sinking Sheila, in spite of the iron tied on her. What good does it do? When they run, they're cooked. And it looks like they're running."

"Where's Bowldersville?"

"Straight down the other side of the Hills, here. About five miles over a secondary road. A bad road."

"That means we got no time."

I found the phone, picked it up. French wasn't at the station. I told the man on duty about the body, spelled out the location for him and instructed him to call George French. He told me to stay where I was which I had no intention of doing at all.

Mickey prowled in the room behind me. I got the Devil's Play Spot, found out real quick that Mrs. Donetti had left with all her belongings.

Then I had it. Every little bit. I asked to talk with Jack Kilgallen and while the connection was being made, Mickey dropped the last piece of the puzzle in place for me.

"Hey, Johnny," he said. "I found a suitcase in the kitchen. Full of clothes."

I turned. "That's it. That's what I've been trying to remember. Sheila had a suitcase when she left Marti Thayer's. It was there all the time."

Mickey came into the hall. "What are you talking about?"

"Nothing," I said. Then to the phone, "Hello, Kilgallen? Berlin. Yeah, never mind the salty dialogue. I need help."

His voice crackled the receiver. "The help you get from me, Berlin, will turn up your toes."

"So you don't like me. But you do like Sheila."

The line buzzed emptily. I thought he'd hung up till I heard the shallow breathing.

He said, "Okay, what's that supposed to mean?"

"She's dead," I said, figuring to get him over it in a hurry. I needed him. "Now you know what she was scared of."

The young voice was ragged. "The dirty rotten ..."

"Easy, kid. I know how you feel. But you can do something about it if you want to."

He sucked a breath that rattled the diaphragm. "What? Just let me know, that's all. Poor kid. All she wanted—"

"All right, all right. We got no time for that. Tell me one thing. You gave Sheila an alibi for the murder of the Teacher girl. I want to know why. And I'm sure she told you."

"She did," he said. "She'd been with Ford. All night. He had another story so she asked me to say I was with her. And I would have been, if she'd let me."

"Thanks, Jack," I said softly. "Thanks a lot."

"Anything I can—"

"Yes. You can get to Bowldersville as fast as you can. I won't guarantee anything except you'll see the end of it.

One way or another."

"I'll be there," he said, and his tone was crisp again. "With a cannon."

I hung up, spun to Mickey. "Let's go."

"Where are we going?"

"To the boat. We can't wait for George or they'll be out into the ocean. Maybe they'll get caught, but that's not good enough. I want it to be now and I want it to be me."

We got into the Buick; its motor was still running.

"How we gonna stop 'em?"

I shook my head. How the hell did I know? I only knew I would—somehow.

We went like a bomb, but I didn't worry about the flashing road, the heaving curves. I was tasting the salt-slap of eating my own ego and I didn't like it at all.

Gina. All the time.

She hadn't given Messner an alibi. He'd given her one.

"Johnny..."

"Yeah, what is it?"

"What was the thing with the suitcase?"

"Sheila had one. When she left Marti Thayer's. I should have seen the connection. It would have made everything clear right away."

"I'm dumb," the hustler said, slitted eyes on the rushing highway. "What's it mean?"

I sighed. "It means they knew I was coming. She had time to pack a bag, or someone packed it for her. The only way they could have known was if you told them, or if they got a call from the only other person who knew I was on my way to Welles."

He glanced at me. "The Donetti broad?"

"The Donetti broad. Get some speed out of this thing."

It was only about nine o'clock, but already Bowldersville was rolled up and tucked in. Mickey briefed me on the place. There was no law, no sheriff's sub-station and, very probably, no telephone. But that didn't make any difference. We slowed through the one-street town, turned off to the fishing-dock area.

It was quiet as a tomb; only the crash of surf and the whining cry of gulls disturbing the dark serenity.

We left the Buick when we ran out of road, walked along the sea wall.

"You know where we're going?"

Mickey shrugged. "I know where Ford keeps his boat. That's what you want, ain't it?"

"That's what I want."

We walked a short fifty yards to where the sea wall split, allowing egress to a long dock, wide, of heavy wood. A shack stood by the near end, a light glowing feebly through a single window. Beyond the shack the pier stretched straight out into the bay, both sides studded with boats of all descriptions in berthing position.

"How far out is it?"

"Not far."

Our footsteps sounded hollowly on the wood; the slap of water against pilings, against boat sides, drowned the wind noise. The night was dark. There were no lights on the pier.

"Watch out for tackle," Mickey said.

I followed his short figure, noticing as we went that some of the boats were not fishing types. There were canvas-shrouded speedboats; gently dipping cruisers, brightly painted and gleaming with chrome. I was glad fog hadn't come up. We'd never have made it the length of the pier.

Mickey stopped. He threw up his arm, ran forward a few paces. He turned, his face a pale blob in the dark.

"It's gone!" he cried. "The *Blue Chip*'s gone!"

I caught his arm. "It can't be. Look close. You sure this is his berth?"

"Here. Right by that big, gray one." He found an upright stanchion, scraped at it. "Look here. See what it says?"

It said, Ford Messner. And I knew I'd lost. The man responsible for the whole stinking mess was safely out to sea. With seventy-five thousand dollars to comfort him if he got moody; and Gina Donetti to warm him if he got cold.

"There's a chance, Johnny. Not much, but a chance anyway."

"What is it? Whatever it is, we'll take it."

"Maybe they moved her in closer. They could anchor in the channel just off the beach at Coley's Club or downhill from the house. For a little while. They couldn't stay there long. But maybe they don't know they have to hurry. Why should they know the body's been found?"

"It's worth a try. Let's go. Run for the car."

Mickey grabbed my arm. "Wait. Here's a boat we can take. Belongs to a friend of mine."

I looked at the open-cockpit speedboat he indicated. It bumped the weathered side of a high-bowed fishing trawler, nets hung on bunting folds over the rail.

"Let's go," I said, jumping for the swaying boat.

The wind had risen. Before long it would be blowing pretty hard. I prayed it would blow up a real storm and keep Ford Messner from chugging out to sea, free of the boil of corruption he'd fostered.

Mickey got the engine started, cursing and pulling at things. Car headlights swirled at the village and a figure came out of the gloom, pounded along the sea wall, down the dock. More headlights stopped behind the first car.

Mickey cast off the lines, threw the boat into reverse and we backed slowly out into the seaway.

"Who is that?"

I pulled the spotlight around, focused it on the pier and hit the switch. Jack Kilgallen ran through the beam, shouting and waving his hands. By now we were ten yards out and in open water.

"Jack!" I shouted. The kid stopped on the pier, waved at us. "No. We got to go! Drive to Coley's Club. Coley's Club! Got that?"

He nodded, started off. Mickey spun the boat out of the seaway, roared around the adjoining pier and into the channel.

"We should have picked him up," he said, shouting over the motor's growl.

"Why?"

"He had a gun. I saw it in his hand."

Mickey hit the throttle. The boat squatted like a happy puppy and surged through the dark water down the spotlight's white path.

We found the *Blue Chip*. If they'd left anybody on it, we'd have been dead. Mickey roared up full throttle, then slacked off, threw the thing in reverse and raced the engine. We stopped like we had brakes, right alongside the cruiser.

Nobody. And nothing. Lights glowed on the thing. But that figured. It was anchored right in the channel, its broad beam blocking all but the smallest craft. I went through the boat, came up empty. Absolutely empty.

Not even a gun.

I hopped back into the speedboat. "Nothing," I told Mickey. "Beach it. We'll hit the club."

The shore was rocky mud flats and sparse bush growth. It sloped gently upward toward the road. We plowed the boat into mud, stuck and waded ashore. We hit the road twenty yards from Coley's Club.

"Lights," Mickey said as we came up to the darker shadow that was the building.

"Where?"

"Other side. I see the glow."

We got around the parking lot, saw a shaft of yellow stabbing from the office window. I slid along the rough side of the building. The cast on my arm hit a drainpipe. We froze. For a moment there was no sound, not even breathing. The voices from inside stopped. Mickey crouched low.

A door opened and Ford Messner's voice came to us, drifting thinly in the dark. "What is it, Mops?"

A thick figure rounded the corner, stared right at us, looked around. Then he turned back. The door slammed. The voices started up again.

"Parisi," Mickey breathed. "Did he see us?"

"No." I crawled toward the window. "Eyes weren't adjusted. Stay there. Be quiet."

I looked inside. The first thing I saw was Gina. She wore a trench coat. The same one I'd first seen her in. She sat on the leather lounge, talking volubly to Messner. Coley O'Rourke was there. And he was a real surprise. He sat at his desk and his suit fit him as badly as ever. But now there were ropes running around his thin body, pinning it to the chair.

Parisi, one arm in a red silk sling, worked clumsily setting a flock of suitcases by the door. Messner was busily transferring money from the desk top to a tan leather attaché case. I listened closely.

They were arguing. About leaving. Messner had the right idea. He knew Sheila would lead to him and no one else. Gina wanted to stick and fight it out. Then Ford said clearly, "Shut the hell up. You want to come, then come. Otherwise, get out of the way. We're leaving now."

I backed out of there, met Mickey in the deep shadow. His eyes glowed.

"What's up?"

I gripped his arm. Tight. He tensed the muscle under my grip. "Hey, Johnny. Take it easy."

"Mickey, listen. They're leaving. We'll have to stop them."

The little crap shooter pulled on me, led me around to the front in the shadow of the rustic porch.

"Listen, Johnny, you gotta unwind. You're like a gambler riding a streak. It's messing up your think-tank. We can't go against guns."

His whispering voice carried sibilantly and my only thought was that they would leave or hear us. I knew enough about the country to know that if they got that cruiser outside the bay entrance, we'd never get them. Maybe somebody else would. But that wasn't good enough for me. Not now.

"Mickey. Here's what we do. It's ten, twelve more minutes from that fishing village to here by the road than it is by boat. Right?"

He nodded.

"All right. Here's the bit. You take off up the road, toward Kilgore. Flag every car. With this joint closed there's no traffic on this road to speak of so the chances are pretty good that the first car will be Jack Kilgallen. You turn him around. Get—"

"Turn him around? You crazy? He's got a rod. At least we'll be able to—"

"No dice. Listen to your Uncle Johnny. Hustle back to the Hills. To Sheila's. By now George French will be there."

"Yeah, but these jerks are ready to leave now. Who's gonna hold Messner till the cops get here?"

I took a breath, watched a flipping reel of my hard-won and stubbornly held values show fleetingly against the lowering night sky. The wind had risen pretty high. It howled. The slap of waves and the clean, sharp smell of the salt air made me aware of how alive I was.

"Who's gonna hold 'em, Johnny? You?"

I grinned in the darkness, tapped the little man with my cast.

"Me," I said. "And my medical bludgeon. Now on your way."

"No, Johnny. I won't let you do that. I'm not going."

"Go on. I'll be all right. If you're back in fifteen minutes, I'll be here. And so will they."

"How you gonna do it?"

"Like Scheherazade. I'm going to walk in there and talk their ears off."

CHAPTER NINETEEN

One thing I forgot. Scheherazade was a woman.

When I walked in that back door without pausing to knock, Gina screamed and Messner almost shot me before I could open my month.

"Hold it!" I said. "For Christ's sake. It's me. Johnny Berlin."

Messner straightened from a shooting crouch, a big .45 clutched in one, long-fingered hand. Gina sat bolt upright on the leather couch, one hand against her mouth. Parisi stood there with his jaw hanging, which was par for the course.

"What do you gain by wasting me?" I asked, closing the door behind me. I lifted my arms slowly out from my sides, the ripped coat sleeve dangling from the arm with the cast on it. I smiled stiffly at Gina. "Wouldn't you think it was a waste, baby?"

"What are you doing here?" Messner asked, lips thinned, white eyebrows high and tight in a bloodless forehead.

I shrugged. "What's the difference? I'm here. Have the ape pat me, see that I'm light. Then I'll tell you a story. And you'll like it."

"What makes you think so, wise guy? What the hell makes you think so?"

Gina said, "Kill him, Ford. Now. Before he gets his wits working."

"You better get yours working. You think I came here alone?"

Messner leaped across the floor. I thought I was a dead man, but the dealer was too shrewd for that. He knew he'd need me if I really had come with help. He jammed the .45 halfway to my backbone, hissed to me that I'd better not move. I didn't. But I wanted to. I wanted to wrap my five good fingers around his lousy neck and squeeze till his head popped off.

"Mops," Messner spat. "The light."

O'Rourke, eyes bulging with the effort of trying to talk through a gag, shook his head at me. I didn't know what that meant. Then the light went out.

"Just stand," the chilly dealer breathed in my ear as the darkness closed around us. "Don't even wiggle. I got nothing to lose now, Berlin. Not nothing. And I'd enjoy killing you."

I swallowed, waited.

"Ford," Gina said, whispering it. "What are we going to do? We're—"

"Shut up, Gina. We got time. No reason why we shouldn't have. Nobody'll think to come here tonight. Maybe tomorrow. After—"

He stopped. "After they find Sheila," I supplied.

He sucked in a breath. The snout of the gun pressed hard into my belly. But he didn't shoot. He relaxed.

"You found her," he said. "Sure. And you came alone. Of course. Gina, call Mops. Tell him it's all right."

"How do you know, Messner?" I said. "How can you be sure?"

He slid away from me in the dark, turned on the light.

"I know," he said. "I know you, Berlin. And I know your kind. That's what you would do. Maybe one other thing. Maybe you'd send somebody for the police. But you wouldn't wait for them. Especially if you saw us getting ready to go, knew we had a boat ready."

Gina rose, tapped across to the door. "Then we've got to get out of here! We've got to move."

She wasn't nervous now, just assured and ready. A little pale, maybe. But she was game. And she made me sick.

Mops came back, reported all clear. Messner nodded. He picked up the tan leather case, glanced around the office.

O'Rourke had started to sweat, great beads jumping out on his forehead.

"That's right, Coley," Messner said. "You, too. You knew that. Why snivel?"

His cold lips broke in a smile. He rubbed a hand quickly over his short hair in a nervous gesture, turned to Mops Parisi.

"Get Berlin over by the wall. When I fire, you let him have it and make sure he's dead. I'll take Coley."

"What do I do?" the woman asked.

"Wait!" It was my voice and I hadn't even thought about speaking. I licked dry lips, worked my shoulders against the wall. It was much too soon for Mickey to have done any good. I knew it. Messner knew it. I said, "Tell me something, dealer. Just one thing."

"I understand, Johnny. You want to get me hung up in a conversation till your help can get here. Whatever it is."

I shook my head, tried to keep my face straight. It felt like a piece of wet, stretched chamois.

"No. A half-minute won't help."

And it wouldn't. He knew that, too. Like he knew everything else. I'd underestimated this man from the beginning. So had everyone. Everyone but Gina. She had an instinct for things like that.

"Okay," Messner finally said. He lowered his gun, waved to Mops. "What's hanging you, Sam Spade?"

"Carla," I said. "I know about Donetti. How you set him up through Gina with the Protective Association bit. Got him to sell his bosses a bill of goods. When the money came, you grabbed it just like you'd always planned. Only you thought the managership of the Play Spot would go with it."

"It would have," Gina said, turning from the window. "If it hadn't been for you."

"Don't blame me. I never would have stuck my nose in except you ran me off the road. You figured I'd been sent along with the money. Mops was on the point, saw Donetti and me drive up together. He called you, chilly. You wheeled out that hearse of Coley's and tried to cream me when I left the Cherbourg."

"Get to it, slicker. You're rambling."

He was getting edgy. He wouldn't go for much more. And it had been but six or seven minutes since Mickey left. Parisi moved in front of me, pushed his gun into my belly.

"Yeah," he said. "Let's go, Ford. Huh, Ford? I want to kill this guy. He cut me. He cut me bad."

His eyes were flat and cold, like dripping coins pulled from salt water.

I swallowed, tried desperately to think. "About Carla. Carla, the kid. What happened to her? Why did she have to—"

Messner turned from the desk. He shifted the attaché case, gripped his weapon.

"I'm sorry about that, Berlin." His pale eyes held mine steadily. "Real sorry. But she heard that damn wop ask for me by name when he drove up to the joint. Driving! The stringy bastard had no business being alive, no business breathing. I plugged him fifty yards from the joint. Fifty yards! What the hell was he—superman? Gina already had the money and all we had to do was get that little—"

He stopped, drew a long breath. "Got me going there, didn't you? Won't work."

"But you were with Sheila when Carla got it. That's how Sheila guessed who really murdered the kid. How could you be so clumsy?"

"It was clumsy. My fault. Gina said I'd better be alibied. So I set one up. With Sheila. Then we discovered that we overlooked one thing. No alibi for Gina. So we switched, with Sheila getting that Indian kid to vouch for her."

"You knew it wouldn't work."

"I know something else." He grinned mirthlessly. "*This* ain't going to work either. But I got no choice."

He nodded to Mops, turned his gun on O'Rourke. This was it, then. The end of a road that began I didn't know where. A road rough and interesting, sometimes good, sometimes frustrating. Now, when I'd found the only important thing that Johnny Twenty-Two had ever recognized, it would end.

It got quiet—just for a heartbeat that seemed to drag and stretch. Mops snicked the safety on his gun, tightened his finger.

"Now, Ford?" His ape face lost all expression, hung inches from mine.

Messner stepped around the desk, put the muzzle of the .45 up to O'Rourke's ear. I caught a flash of something at the window, heard glass break. I leaped to the side and slammed my left hand into Parisi's face, forgetting the cast.

Shots roared out and glass shattered and all hell broke loose in the small confines of the office. Parisi stumbled back, his mouth a mess, trying to bring up the gun. A bullet hit his head as I watched, spun it, a crimson smear appearing as if by magic.

"Stand still!"

It was a shout from outside the window. Messner stood, bent at the hips, the .45 drooping from lax fingers. A burst of shots chattered from the window. Messner jerked with the sound, spun and fell to the floor. His face was toward me; one of his white eyebrows had become a red hole.

Gina screamed. She broke from the far wall, ran for the door. She might have made it, too. But she stopped in midstride, scooped at the attaché case trapped under Messner's arm. I shook the paralysis and dove for her, hit the flying trench coat right behind the knees. Her head snapped forward hard against the door.

For a little time there was no sound. I lay on the floor, my head resting on the softness of Gina Donetti, wondering how I could still be alive and how Mickey had made the trip so fast.

But he hadn't. A voice from the door, an urban, cultured, very precise voice told me different.

"Mr. Berlin. I told you to let me know."

I rolled over. My cast banged on the floor. The room was a mess. In the doorway stood Horace Atkinson Gilbertson, the knobby-muscled kid beside him. At the window was the grinning face of Mare, the big-nosed hoodlum. Everybody had a gun.

Mickey broke through the door, rushed to me.

"Jesus, Johnny, did you have to shave it so fine?"

"Me shave it fine?" I struggled up. I felt drained, emptier than a loser's pockets and blacker than his scowl. "I still don't believe I'm alive."

"Here, let me help." He got me onto the couch, and I leaned back, closed my eyes. Mickey said, "I met Kilgallen all right. But right behind him was this guy. With his private army. So he busts down on us on the highway, says let's go straight to the rescue." Mickey smiled, pushing up his half-apple cheeks. "Like the Marines, man. We been outside the door for five minutes."

I groaned. "Five minutes."

A siren growled far away, grew in the night. Cops. Coming hell bent. I looked a question at Gilbertson.

"We sent Kilgallen while we came on," he said. "I told you once, Berlin. Where it's possible, I operate strictly within the law."

I nodded. "How about the money?"

He sighed, handed his little snub-nose .38 to Marc, who'd entered quietly, stood with an efficient-looking Schmeisser machine-pistol gripped in his arms.

"I'll claim it. And I'll get it. But I believe the operation at the lake is done."

"I'm glad," I said.

"You should be. Here are McKaneville's finest. Out of their jurisdiction, incidentally."

Sirens screamed into the parking lot, died growling as their cars slid to stops. Horns and lights; barked orders and staccato footsteps. It took quite a while to get order restored. Mickey disappeared and I had to answer a million questions. French was up on most of it so I just had to explain the part he hadn't seen. But it still took a while. By the time we got straightened around to where he'd even think about letting me go, it was midnight.

"One thing, slicker," French said, smiling tightly. "Who do we tag for the kid? For Carla?"

"Yeah," I said. I leaned forward, stared at Gina Donetti, conscious now, leaning against the wall, feet doubled under her. Her eyes came up to mine. "Messner's dead. Gina could tell you he wasn't at the lake during the murder period and that would make him guilty. But that isn't the way it was."

Gina said, "Johnny," very softly and there was no mistaking the abject promise. "Johnny, please ..."

I shook my head at her, let her look real hard at my eyes. She slumped against the wall, legs sprawled and began to cry silently.

French took my arm. "What's the story? Make it short, but make it complete."

"Okay. I'm just beat, George, that's all. Tired and hurt and sick to God-damn death of people." The rookie cop handed me a lit cigarette. I nodded, took it. "This broad ramrodded the whole thing. I'll slice it up briefly. You can sweat O'Rourke there for the details. He heard the whole thing here. And I suspect he found out more than he should have somewhere along the line. They were going to kill him, anyway, so they probably had a reason."

"That's right, Lieutenant," O'Rourke said. He was still white, holding with trembling hands to the flask Horace Gilbertson had provided. "I knew for days Ford killed Donetti. But I didn't dare do anything. I didn't dare. He told—"

"All right," French said. "Go ahead, Johnny. Tell."

"The Gambling Protective thing was just a gimmick. Gina talked her old man into thinking it was a good idea, sicked him

onto Messner. They whacked out a plan. Then Donetti took it
to his bosses." I nodded to the banker, gunless now, along with
his two hoodlums. Jack Kilgallen stood beside him. "This guy is
one. They liked the idea, knew it would take local action to get
anything done, so they told Donetti to go ahead."

"On his own initiative, Lieutenant," Gilbertson said. "Make
no mistake about that."

"Yeah, all right." French backed to the desk, stepping around
the chalked spaces on the floor where the bodies had been. He sat
on the edge. "How'd he do for Donetti?"

"You told me," I said. "That doniker window. All right, bath-
room, men's room, whatever." French smiled. "He met Donetti
away from the club. They were secret partners, it was natural to
be secretive. Ford shoots him, runs like a dog back to the club
and almost gets run over by the Cadillac ramming into the lot.
At the same moment at the Play Spot, Gina was appropriating
the money. The seventy-five thousand for expenses. Donetti just
didn't die quick enough. Messner was around the corner on his
way back when the car hit. He heard Donetti tell the girl, "Get
Ford Messner. The dirty Johnny Ronce!" just as he was kicking. I
heard the last part."

French grunted. "Why didn't she tell us right away?"

"Ford. He ran around the club, came up as I was trying to get
the kid straightened out. He was a pretty chilly guy, George. He
scared the kid. And kept on scaring her. He ran into her the night
she got killed in the Cherbourg and told her to be careful, to stay
home and mind her business, or something like that. She threw a
wingding in the club. I put her in a cab."

I stopped, turned my eyes toward the woman on the floor.
She didn't look sexy any more. She looked sad. Her hair fell
forward down her face and great, rolling tears carried mascara
down her cheeks.

"Gina killed her. She knew Carla wouldn't go near Messner
so she picked the girl up at her home when the cab got there.

Told her she had a message from Laddy Layton. Then ran over her. Only thing that makes sense. Otherwise there was no need to kill Sheila. When Sheila got it and I realized that Marti Thayer and that punk Frank knew I was coming to Welles, I knew Gina was the connection. Before that it was a little hard for me. I was playing hearts with the tramp."

I looked up from my burning cigarette; French's eyes were on the door. I turned. Fran was there with Mickey System. Her face was twisted and for a moment I thought she would cry. But she didn't. She walked straight to me, held my face in both hands.

"Oh, Johnny..."

"Hi," I said. "My suit isn't back from the cleaners, but if you wait a few minutes you can drive me home. Okay?"

She nodded, eyes brimming suddenly. "Okay. I'll wait outside."

Her eyes found the huddled figure against the wall. She squeezed my shoulder hurtingly. I patted her.

"Go, woman," I said gently.

She sniffled, smiled through the tears.

"Gone," she said.

French finished inspecting his shoe sole. His eyes were a little bleak. He moved his lips in a small smile.

"You make a pretty good detective, slicker. You see any implications for O'Rourke?"

The skinny guy cried out, but French cut him off with an arm wave.

"No," I said. "He just likes to play gangster. He kept Messner around because he had eyes for Sheila." I shrugged. "You know how that goes. And he probably would have gone on being a good dog if they hadn't killed her. Sheila goofed when she called me. Then Messner knew he had to shut her up. I don't know who actually held the knife. Maybe Coley does. Anyway, get the rest from him, will you? I'm beat and I got a ride waiting for me."

"Sure, Johnny."

French pointed at Gilbertson. "I want statements from you people. And you'll be under technical arrest. With Berlin's testimony, there's no way we can hold you. But I want you to know I would if there was a way."

Gilbertson nodded, almost bowed. "Quite right, Mr. French. Your duty. You might like to know that I'm recommending our operation at the lake be terminated."

"I might," French agreed. "There's some things I want from you yet, Johnny. But they can wait. Go ahead."

I said, "There's one thing I'd like to know. Horace—" I turned to the banker. "How the hell did you get here in time to keep me from getting my pretty head ventilated?"

He smiled, rubbed a knuckle over his gray brush. "Like a movie, eh, Johnny?"

"Yeah. A bad movie. What's the pitch?"

"We were behind Kilgallen all the way. When your call came to him at the Play Spot, I was notified. He borrowed a gun from Marc. We followed. All the way. To the quaint little village and then up that impossible road to the Kilgore Hills. Finally, here. After meeting Mickey on the road, very simple."

"Well, I won't knock it. It kept me alive. And I have a special reason for wanting to be alive right now. Couple things, George. When Donetti left that message for me at the Club Carroll, he probably wanted to find out if I really had been sent by the syndicate to protect the money. He didn't care. He could have used the help. Messner knew about the call through Gina. He sicked her onto me. That's why he set up the kill at the Club Carroll. He could have killed the guy anywhere. But that was the only place he'd told me to meet him. Where he knew I'd be. He figured me for a patsy."

"Not so far wrong," French said. "I was fitting you for it pretty good all along. Only Fran's insistence that it couldn't have been you kept me from locking you up and trying to prove it. So you're lucky in more ways than one, slicker."

"I know, George...I want you to know, I mean, the way it turned out..."

He grunted, slab face twisting away. "Yeah. All right. Go ahead. Get out of here."

My legs held me. I wouldn't have bet on it. I felt funny. Not funny ha-ha, funny peculiar. The ground was there beneath my feet and yet it wasn't. And I was tired. So Goddamn tired.

Gina looked up as I rose, began cursing me in a low, harsh voice. Her eyes were wild.

"Sure, baby," I said softly. "Sure."

"You didn't have to throw me, Johnny, you bastard!" she sobbed. "You didn't have to."

"Yeah, I did, Gina. I really did."

I got out the door as quickly as I could. There was a deep silence behind me, punctuated only by the racking sobs of the woman.

The car radio played softly and Fran drove carefully, just barely rolling. The night was still black and starless, without fog, and no mist had blown in. Fran's little coupe was warm and tight and I lay back against the seat and let the accumulated tensions run out of me.

"Hell of a thing," I said to the ceiling. "Johnny Berlin playing cop. They'd never believe it in Vegas."

Fran reached out her hand, turned my head. "Who cares?" she said, voice husky with unshed tears.

"Yeah. Who does?"

I watched the play of moonlight on her face, her breasts as she drove. Beautiful. But not cold. Not cold at all. Her lips tilted up at the corners and she blushed under my look. She glanced at me, back to the road.

"Well? No funny dialogue? No snappy lines to amuse and confuse?"

I reached across my body, clumsy because of the cast, gripped her arm. "Stop the car," I said.

"But Johnny, we have to get home. You're hurt."

"Stop the God-damn car!"

She did. And I wasn't hurt that badly.

I wasn't hurt at all.

THE END

ABOUT THE AUTHOR

Elmer Merle Parsons aka "Philip Race" was born in Pittsburgh, PA in 1926. In 1949, when he was 23 years old, he was convicted of burglary and grand theft for stealing a car from a Phoenix used car lot and leading police on a wild chase that ended in a crash. He served three years in Chino State Prison...but didn't stay free for long. In 1955, he was arrested in Pasadena, CA for passing 22 stolen checks, which he told the court he needed to "tide him over" while awaiting money for a script he claimed he'd sold and because he couldn't get a job due to his prison record. He was sentenced to five years in prison, which he served at San Quentin, where he became editor of the prison newspaper and sold his first novel, "Self-Made Widow," to Fawcett for $3500 advance under the pen-name "Philip Race." He wrote & published two more novels, "Killer Take All" and "Johnny Come Deadly," under his pen name and one western, "Texas Heller," under his own name. After his release in 1960, he wrote one novel ("Dark of Summer") and several westerns ("Fargo," "The Easy Gun") under his own name and also contributed scripts for many TV series, including *Sea Hunt, Cheyenne, Ripcord, Bonanza, The Dakotas, The Virginian* and *Flipper.*

www.ingramcontent.com/pod-product-compliance
Lightning Source LLC
Chambersburg PA
CBHW022200240626
47153CB00007B/2755